SHHH' IT'S THE BILL COLLECTOR

Suzy Q

Order this book online at www.trafford.com
or email orders@trafford.com

Most Trafford titles are also available at major online book retailers.

Printed in the United States of America.

ISBN: 978-1-4669-1085-0 (sc)
ISBN: 978-1-4669-1087-4 (hc)
ISBN: 978-1-4669-1086-7 (e)

Library of Congress Control Number: 2012900058

Trafford rev. 04/19/2012

 www.trafford.com

North America & international
toll-free: 1 888 232 4444 (USA & Canada)
phone: 250 383 6864 ♦ fax: 812 355 4082

CONTENTS

DEDICATION

To my deceased mother Helena Blackwell who continues to guide
me from above with her spirit and Christian memories.
Everyday still is Mother's Day for me!
Then to my husband Lawrence, and my children Gaffney Jr.,
Michael and Maurice Hargis, I thank and love you!
Much love to my Sisters' Cassandra, Ann, Jerry Lynn, and Darlene.
To my two brothers' Reverend Dennis and Jeffrey Blackwell,
Love you!
To my special (Road Dogs) nieces Katrina and Amirah,
and Baby Gaffney, you are loved.
Then to all other family members I thank you for your support.
To all of my friends who continue to encourage me and support me
through prayer, words of encouragement and for buying my books.
I thank and love all of you. I ask that you continue to keep me in
prayer. Prayerfully more is yet to come!
A special thank you to my Prayer Warriors, Esther Parrish, Donna
Parrish and Lynnaye Winters, who also share my vision.
I would be remised if I did not thank all of the people who have been
hassled by Bill Collectors, telemarketers and any unwanted calls,
for having the courage and faith to trust and believe in God
by keep holding on.
There is a bight side somewhere and joy does come in the morning!

ACKNOWLEDGEMENTS

I want to first acknowledge God who is first and foremost in my life! Through his vision, grace and mercy I was able to write this Christian Novel. I acknowledge that it is his will and blessing for me to tell my stories in a Christian way. I can do all things through Christ who strengthens me! I thank you God for being so awesome in my life!

I also give honor to God who saw it fit to allow me to retire and get well so that I could continue to write Christian Novels and to also work on my PhD as well. *He said by his stripes I am healed* Isaiah 53:5

I again want to acknowledge all people who have been harassed by bill collectors, telemarketers or who receives any unwanted phone calls.

Many of you who are reading this book can relate to similar situations such as this.

If you are being harassed by bill collectors ask them to stop calling you and ask them to send their request for payments or any correspondence by mail. If they refused to stop calling, get there names and find out who their superior is and let them know what is happening. If this does not work contact a legal authority or a Television News Station.

It is also very important that you keep all receipts and important documents in a safe place for at least five years. Many times you have bill collectors that will try and harass for bills that you have already paid.

In this economic time of hardship, many people will be unable to pay their bills and mortgages; and they will be harassed by mean and disrespectful bill collectors. Many times you can't see your way clear and you are at your wits end.

Friends please know that help is on the way! So hold on.

Please know that God does answer prayer. And prayer is a very strong and viable vehicle for some peace!

INTRODUCTION

Sandra is a gorgeous African American Woman. She also is a single divorced mother who is raising three sons and a grandson. She and her husband divorced ten years ago. Sandra not only is gorgeous but she also is the nicest person to have in your life. They don't come any nicer than Sandra. Even in the situation that she is in, Sandra would do anything for you!

Ever since the divorce she has been supporting the boys on her own. Her ex-husband never gave them support financially or as a father. She has had to play mother and father to them at all times. She has grown to love her parenting roles. And she loves her boys with all her heart and soul. Michael is 15 years old, Wayne is 13 years old and Anthony who is her baby son is 11 years old. She has very handsome sons. They are very obedient and they love their mother as much as she loves them. Her grandson Trippy is six years old. Trippy is cute as a button. His mother Cheryl passed away two years ago from Multiple Sclerosis at the age of twenty six. Then Sandra got custody of him. She adores Trippy, he has been the love of her life. He keeps Sandra laughing all of the time. Sandra said she doesn't know what she would do if Trippy wasn't with her.

However at times she has had to work two jobs just to give her boys a good Christian life. Thank God for her family who has been very supportive and helps her with babysitting and finances when needed. She and her family live in a small town "Louisville" outside of Florida. Sandra also has very good friends who always has her and her families' back.

Even though Sandra could have gotten another man in her life; she decided that she would take care of the children, putting them first. She didn't want to have men in and out of their lives. She saw how so many women had men in and out of their lives which caused so many problems for their children. Sandra was determined that her children would get a good Christian upbringing even if she had to sacrifice her needs.

Today there are so many women who can relate to Sandra and her situation. And just like Sandra they too can survive as long as they have Faith in God!

FRIDAY NIGHT

EVERYONE IS AT SANDRA'S HOUSE in her basement for their regular Friday night party. The music was jumping with Casanova by Gerald Levert playing. A loud knock comes on the door. Hey Sandra someone is knocking on the door, do you want me to get it. Sandra softly replies while waving her hand to turn the music down. Be quiet I think it's the Bill Collector. Sandra slowly walks upstairs and goes to the window and looks out. She tip toes back downstairs to her friends and whispers its the Bill Collector. "We have to be real quiet until he leaves". They all sat down on the floor trying to be quiet. Michael looked at Trina trying to make her laugh. Trina put her hands over her mouth so that she wouldn't laugh out loud. Sandra stared at her friends with her hands on her hips, while glaring at them with them with a don't mess with me look on her face.

The Bill Collector knocked a little while longer. Then he began talking to himself. "I know they in there". They think I'm stupid. I'm going to get her yet. You just wait and see he mumbled to himself! Finally the Bill Collector slowly walks away clinching his fists as he gets into his car. He revved up his car and pulled off.

Trippy looked out the window and saw him drive off down the street. Then Trippy runs over to Sandra and whispers in her ear "Nanny he's gone, he just pulled off. While he was driving in his car, he began ringing her phone. Sandra hollers out to her children to let the phone

1

ring, I know who it is she said. It's the Bill Collector. Now he's being a pain.

She said softly under her breath.

Then Sandra hollers out, put some music on and lets party. Marvin Gaye's Party song was on. Anthony shouted it's a party over here.

Brenda got up and said come on Anthony let's dance. Everybody got up to dance.

The music was pumping loud and the party was high. Joe had the tambourines in the background playing to the beat. Lynn was blowing a whistle. What a time everyone was having.

The guest started a soul train line dancing to the beat of Flashlight, by the Ohio Player. Then the party people pulled out all kinds of old dance moves. It was funny to see some of the ole heads trying to bust some moves. Brenda went down to do a split and actually split her pants. They were doing the robot, mash potatoes, twist, chicken, popcorn and penguin. What a time, what a time they were having. They were all laughing so hard and crying at the same time.

Just as the last dancer went down the soul train dance line, a loud steady booming knock comes on the door. Everyone was in rare form; laughing, dancing and having so much fun. Guess who it was? "It was the Bill Collector back again"! Sandra said just let him knock until he gets tired or his knuckles gets raw. Sandra's friends kept on partying. They simply ignored his knocking!

Finally the Bill Collector went back to his car and started blowing up her telephone again. But no one would answer it. After awhile he gave up. "That woman makes me so mad he said mumbling to himself". But I'm not going to give up. "I will get her if this is the last thing I do".

After partying for awhile, everyone sat down so they could eat. Whew dancing sure makes me hungry said Brenda. Ah girl that's all you do! I heard that Trina. Yawl stop talking about me whined Brenda.

Oh Brenda we're just having a little fun!

Sandra what did you fix to eat? She came swishing out in the living room with her hands on her hip and with her thin lips pershed into a point. Yawl know I cooked a little bit of everything; fried fish, ribs, chicken wings, potato salad, seafood salad, collard greens, cornbread and some sweet tea. You're making me hungry and I'm ready to eat now, whined Larry. Sandra please fix me a plate? Ah you can fix your own plate, I don't know what you want to eat. I want some of everything, he replied. I thought you would get me a plate! Now, now, lets stop fighting there plenty for everyone to eat. It was so quiet while they ate, that you could hear a pin drop. Girl you sure put your foot in preparing this food, Joe said licking his lips and fingers. You know I want to take me a plate home. "Joe you know you're good for a take home plate. He always want a takeout plate. Like that's something new. Man you take a plate home every Friday. You know you don't have to ask". Ah Trina be quiet. Trina laughs and said "Joe you know I'm playing with you. I know you love to eat, especially when Sandra cooks".

This is good Nanny! Thank you Trippy.

After eating everyone went back to partying. The music was pumping even louder and harder. They all had full bellies and was ready to party all night long.

Sugar Hill, Cool Moo d, Dougie Fresh, The Ohio Players, Stevie Wonders, Johnny Gill, Teddy Pendergrass, The Commodores, Tina Marie, Patti La Belle and the Average White Band songs were played. The crowd partied all night long. Finally one by one they began to leave. See you next Friday night Sandra, we had a blast everyone said as they left. Bye yawl, I'll see you next week.

Andrea was the last one to leave the party. Before leaving she asked Sandra what was going on with this Bill Collector Guy. Sandra sat down and began to weep. Girl this man calls and comes around all the time harassing me for a bill. And you know Andrea this fool has even started harassing me on my job. All of my co-workers knows how he's harassing me, and they finally told him that I didn't work there anymore. Girl he's making my life a living hell. He just won't let up!

It's the constant calls and visits to my home, over and over again. He calls every day, and comes to the house knocking every day, knocking like a real crazy mad man. Sandra throws her hands up and says I can't take it anymore. But what can I do? We have named him the Crazy Bill Collector, because he just doesn't let up. He calls and comes to the house day and night! It almost seems like he has something personal against me. We have to disguise our voice or say wrong number when he calls. Now it's gotten so bad that we don't even answer the phone anymore.

We just look at the caller ID and let the phone ring. Most of the times it is him. He's ring until he gets tired.

Andrea, I pay what I can but it's never enough. They can't get blood out of a stone. I don't know what to do. Andrea you know last year a week after Mother's Day, he called and had the nerve to ask me didn't I get any monetary gifts for mother's day. Then he wanted know how I supported myself and paid my bills. He also said "well you paid the last payment with a Visa Card, I know you have money". What nerve of him! I had to get with him and tell him that he needed to stop harassing me and asking me those kind of questions. I told him that he was overstepping him boundaries, and that I was going to report him. What did he say. He just hung up on me!

It's depressing to have to always look over my shoulders before I go out. I don't know why he is hounding me so much. I wonder if I'm his only client. Girl sometimes I disguise my voice to sound like a foreigner, other times I would say wrong number. Andrea his calls are non-stop. It's a good thing that we have caller id. We always know when he's calling because his number almost always shows up. He's even tried to get slick, so now when he calls, the called id will show privet number. When it shows privet number we don't even pick the phone up.

Sandra have you tried to call his supervisor. Because girl this sounds like he's really harassing you. You don't have to take that. Andrea my nerves are so shot I wouldn't even know what to say to a supervisor. His calls is causing me to have bad stomach pains. I can't sleep at night and I'm always watching my back. I don't want to go out anymore. If I didn't have to go work I wouldn't go out at all. The house parties give me some relief and some sanity.

And you know Andrea the crazy thing about this whole situation is that this isn't even my bill. This is a bill that my ex—husband made and wouldn't pay. It's not my bill. Sandra breaks down and started to sob.

Because my ex-husband does not work and the collectors can't find him they want me to pay it. She breaks down again and cries saying it's just not fair. I have to live too! I'm too afraid to go out and have fun, that's why I have my parties here. This isn't the first time that my ex—husband stuck me with a bill. When we first broke up, my ex husband quit his job. He got his 401k savings fund and spent it without giving me or the boys any money. He failed to pay taxes on it. A few years later the IRS taxed my wages for six months because we were still married, even thought we filed separately. I haven't even gotten over that situation. Now the Bill Collector is doing me the same way. It's just not fair. It's not fair at all.

Andrea walks over and hugs Sandra and said don't cry girl we are going to find a way to work it out. And you're not gonna stayed hemmed up in your house. We are going to go out and have some fun. Andrea looks at Sandra and said very sternly, you are going to start living your life again. Right now you are just existing and not living your life! Do you hear me. Look at me Sandra. Do you hear me. We're going to work this thing out! Okay Andrea! Thanks for listening to me. Sandra that's what friends are for.

"Sweetie I "gatta" run but I'll be talking with you real soon". They embraced and Andrea left.

After cleaning up and putting things back in order, Sandra sat down on the sofa and started to brainstorm. She finally fell fast asleep on the sofa, this matter had really drained her.

SLEEP

It was 3:00 am when something woke Sandra up. She was having a bad night mare. He's here she thought, I have to hid. After completely waking up and looking around she realized that she was safely in her home. Why am I letting this get the best of me she wondered. This is starting to consume me. I've gotta find a way to work this out, please Lord help me she cried out. Sandra put her slippers on and slowly walked upstairs to bed.

Sandra finally dozed off into a peaceful sound sleep. It was 5:00 am when she woke up. She hadn't meant to sleep that late. Sandra was trying to get to her 6:00 a.m. prayer meeting. She came downstairs and turned the TV on. Sandra always went to prayer every morning, Monday through Friday. I need to get up and shower. Oh how I need prayer very badly she whispered. I really need to get to the alter and have a talk with God. I can't wait, she said!

Sandra got down on her knees and began to pray.

"Dear Lord please, hear my prayers. I'm starting to suffer real bad.
My stomach and head hurt all of the time. I can't sleep, and I'm
afraid to go out of my house. I feel like a prisoner in my own home.
Lord I can't pay this bill so I'm asking you to help me. God please
send me some help! Show me what I need to do.
Lord I thank you. Amen!

With tears in her eyes Sandra laid down on the sofa. This has really been very stressful on her. She began having migraine headaches over this situation. What am I going to do she ask herself with tears running down her face, what am I going to do?

As she laid there, Grandmother Elaine rang the phone. Hello yes, grandmother. Baby what's wrong, I can hear it in your voice that something is wrong. Grandmother I'm feeling so low today. This Bill Collector situation has really gotten me down. I have such a terrible headache. Baby I knew something was wrong. I was looking for you today in church at 6:00 am prayer. When you didn't show up I knew something had to be wrong. Sandra you never miss 6:00 am prayer.

Sandra you need to get yourself together and not let this affect you anymore. Everyone is in debt these days and owes bills. You can't let this ruin your life.

Baby are you going to church tomorrow morning. Yes Grandma. Honey I'm coming over to take the boys and Trippy for a couple of hours today! They can eat dinner at my house. This way you can get some sleep. I will call Michael and let him know I am on my way. Thanks Grandma. Sandra you don't have to thank me, this is what family does. Yes Grandma, I love you! I love you too baby and everything is going to be alright!

The boys were old enough to get dressed and take care of themselves. Michael, Wayne and Anthony could also cook if they had to. Today they would be in for a treat. Grandmother was a great cook. She spoiled the boys and made them whatever they wanted to eat. She loved them so very much.

The boys also knew to come in the house and lock up once they returned from Great Grandmother's house. Sandra had raised them well. They were good sons. She loved them very much and they loved and adored her.

They were having such a great time that Great Grandmother Elaine let them spend the night. This meant pop corn and late night movies for them. The boys ran and gave Great Grand mom Elaine a big hug and kiss. We love you Grand mom they said. She felt that Sandra could use the rest to help get her nerves calmed down. This Bill Collector situation was now starting to worry Grandmother Elaine. She hated seeing her grand daughter upset and worried like she was.

SUNDAY MORNING

MICHAEL, HIS BROTHERS AND TRIPPY came home the next morning from Great Grandmother Elaine's house. Sandra was still sleep on the couch so they decided to let her sleep until 6:30 am. Anthony woke Sandra up at 6:30. Mom it's time to get up. Are you going to church today he asked? Whew I must have been tired she said as she stretched out her arms. I had a good night sleep. It's just what the Doctor ordered. I need to do this more often, I really do she said. Son let me get up and get myself ready for church.

Mikey was I sleep out here all night? Yes Mom, when we came in this morning and saw you sleeping, you look so peaceful, so I covered you with the blanket and let you sleep. Mom you were even cooing in your sleep like a little baby. (coo, coo, coo) Mom that was funny. Ah hush boy, mind your business now. She told him.

Anthony came into the living room and said "Mom" we are cooking breakfast for you! Sandra sat up on the sofa and said you children are so good to me, I love. Okay let me get up so I can wash my face and brush my teeth. I'll be in the kitchen very shortly.

She turns and smiles and then said come here my children, come to Momma. She gathers them in her arms and gives them the biggest hug. Wait, wait for me Trippy calls out as he comes running. Nanny I want a hug too. She leans down and give him a hug. I love you too Trippy she said. I love you too Nanny then he plants a big kiss on her cheek.

Sandra looks up and said, *"Thank You Lord"*. In all that she goes through, her three sons and grandson bring her joy and they help her to see that there is a bright side somewhere. These guys were her life.

As she began to brush her teeth she remember something her mother always said and that is, *"trouble don't last always", and the joy of the Lord is my strength"*.

Sandra said out loud yeah that's right "trouble don't last always".

She also remember her mother saying to her that:

> *"God don't put more on you that you can't bear".*

But you know sometimes Sandra felt like her shoulders were sore because the load was just little too heavy for her to bear.

After breakfast Sandra took her shower and prepared herself for church. Even though she trusted and believed in the Lord she always was looking out for that Bill Collector. The boys were sitting in the living room all ready waiting for Sandra. She looked out her window before running to the car. Hurry, hurry up boys, run to the car. We don't want the Bill Collector to get us. The coast was all clear. Sandra and the boys jumped in her car and rode off to church. As they rode to church Sandra sent up a silent prayer.

> *Thank you Jesus, thank you Jesus! she said.*

Then she began to sing to the boys, Jesus loves me this I know, for the Bible tells me so, little ones to him belong they are weak but he is strong. The boys listened quietly as she sang. Yes Jesus loves me, yes Jesus loves me, yes Jesus, loves me for the Bible tells me so.

Then the boys began to giggle to themselves. They really didn't know the effect the Bill Collector was having on their Mom. But they knew Sandra could sing. By the time Sandra had finished the last verse she was pulling up to the church. Whew that didn't take long at all. She parked the car and they got out and walked to the front of the church.

CHURCH/CHOIR

SANDRA AND HER FAMILY WALKED all the way down front and sat in the pews where they sat every Sunday morning. Sandra and her family got in church just before the choir marched in. This Sunday the church was full because it was Homecoming Sunday. And all of the choir members were in the choir. Most of them had been away on vacation and now they were all back. And they sound real good too as they marched in.

The congregation stood and recited the call to worship listed in their church bulletins. Praise and worship was so spiritual this Sunday. It seemed like everyone has something to praise God for.

After the scriptures were read. Pastor Dennis acknowledge all of the visitors by having them stand, and say where they were from, allowing them to say something about God. There were quite a few visitors in attendance, and many of them stood and gave testimonies. Just when you think you were going through something, and then you listen to someone else's problems everything seemed to be alright.

Once the Praise dancers began to dance the parishioners got on their feet. These young dancers were so blessed and anointed. And they always blessed someone whenever they danced. Today Sandra knew she was being blessed by the praise dancers. Her mind was stayed on Jesus and his goodness. She felt like her burdens were being lifted.

The Praise Dancers were a ministry all by themselves. The boys always enjoyed the praise dancers. Every Sunday they presented a new dance that uplifted your spirits. These five dancers were so spiritual and gifted at such a young age. Most of all they loved the Lord!

Trippy always enjoyed offering time, because he held the basket for the Sunday School. This made him feel grownup and important. He stood so tall and proud as he held the basket. Trippy also loved Sunday School which was held on Saturdays. He always came home and shared what he learned in class with Sandra and his uncles. He even tried to preach to us when he got home. Trippy liked and remembered everything that the preacher said every Sunday. Even though he was six years old, he loved the Lord! He always said that when he grew up he wanted to be a preacher.

The word in the Bible said "Train up a Child in the way he should go: and when he is old he will not depart from it. (*Proverbs 22*:6) Sandra believed in this proverb and she did her best to make sure that she brought them up in a Christian upbringing.

After the offering and offertory was done, Reverend Dennis asked the parishioners' to remain standing and meet and greet their neighbors.

It was good to see everyone, because many of the parishioners had also taken the summer off for vacations. It seemed like they had been gone forever. There was a lot of hugging and kissing in the service that morning. Oh what a time, what a time they had.

The choir stood up and started singing "How Great is Our God". They sang with so much enthusiasm and joy, which really moved the congregation. Everyone was up on their feet shouting, praising God and singing along with the choir.

How Great is our God?
How Great, How Great is our God!
You're the name above all names
You are worthy to be praised
And our hearts will sing
How Great is our God!

Pastor Dennis got up and said the Lord is truly in this service today, and the word seems to be already brought through the music, so I guess I can sit down. I'll just say Amen! Someone shouted Pastor give us the word, give us the word, we want to hear the word. Pastor Dennis we still need the word! He stood tall in the pulpit sending up praises himself. Yes congregation we serve a awesome God and his word must be told to a dying world. Saints this morning the spirit has moved me to bring a different word other than what I had planned to bring. I want to tell you that I'm thankful, yes I'm thankful for you see he woke me up this morning and placed my feet on solid ground and started me on my way. Yes Saints of God, I am very thankful, so very thankful, hallelujah!

Before Reverend Dennis could say another word the church erupted in thankful praise. They were praising and shouting; and the musicians were playing to the spirit. Oh what a time what a time.

Finally as they quieted down a bit Reverend Dennis got up and said,

The sermon this morning is:
Do you believe in miracles?

Some of the parishioners were still shouting and praising God, saying yes we do! When the church finally settled down.

Reverend Dennis said "Good morning church". Please bow your heads for prayer so that we can go to the throne of grace.

My hope is built on nothing less than Jesus blood and righteousness.
I dare not trust the sweetest frame but I'm going to holy lean on Jesus
name. On Christ the solid rock I stand all other
ground is sinking sand.
Father God this morning we thank you for your grace and mercy.
We thank you for your redeeming power and love. God we thank
you for your holy spirit. We ask that you rain down afresh on us this
morning. We ask that you save and anoint anyone standing in the
need of your power, grace and mercy.
Then Father I ask that you Let the words in my mouth and the
meditation of my heart be acceptable in your sight, Oh Lord my
strength, redeemer and savior. In Jesus name we say
Amen!

Pastor Dennis said that in order to believe in God's miracles you must have faith. He said faith is what moves God. Just ask and he'll hear you. He said knock on the door and he'll open it. He said seek me and you'll find me. Pastor Dennis said when you go to God, go to him earnestly and ask out of your heart and God will hear and answer you. Pastor Dennis said "that in all that we do, we must first give God Praise, because if we don't the rocks will cry out"! "Yes we need to trust God more and ourselves less, Saints, so that we can give God our total praise"!

This message really moved Sandra this morning. She felt the spirit moving in her soul. Then the choir sang a medley of songs. The choir was on fire this morning and Sandra couldn't sit still any longer. She got up from her seat and began to shout, giving praise and thanking God. She didn't know that she caused the whole congregation to start shouting. Everyone was shouting and praising God. All of a sudden Pastor Dennis jumped off of the pulpit and began shouting and running up and down the aisles. What a joy what a joy divine.

After everyone calmed down Pastor Dennis said "To *God be the Glory*",. Then he said but I just can't leave this place this morning without an alter prayer. It's seems that this morning we are all standing in the need of prayer. We all need a special word and touch from God.

This Sunday morning there just happened to be a visiting minister in the congregation worshiping with them. Pastor Dennis asked him to come to the pulpit and do the alter prayer. Reverend Lawrence said he would come and lead us in prayer. Praise God Reverend Dennis, I will be obedient to the spirit. Yes I will.

Reverend Lawrence got up and said "the alter is now open for prayer. Church I feel that there is someone here who is carrying a heavy burden and is really standing in the need of prayer". Come one, come all, he said. We will wait until you come. This morning we are all looking for God to move and change hearts and situations. Sandra and her family came to the alter for prayer. Almost all of the whole church including Pastor Dennis came to the alter. There was so much praise and worship and tears flowing in the church, before Reverend Lawrence started the prayer. He said truly the spirit of the Lord is in this house of worship today. Everyone was on a heavenly high.

As they settled down, Pastor Lawrence said, I want everyone who can to kneel at the alter to do so, and the ones who can't kneel to join hands with someone standing next to you while bowing your heads.

> *"Father God we come one more time to give you praise. Father this is the day that you have made and we are glad to be in it. Father we come this morning with heavy hearts and lifting up our partitions to you. But first we want to thank you. Father we thank you because you have been our bridge over trouble waters, and our shelter in the times of storms. Father you are a good and just God, and we say thank you! Father you been better to us then we've been to you. So we say thank you. We thank you for your grace and your mercy. Now Father as you continue to shower your blessings on us, we say thank you! We ask you to surround this alter and church. We ask that you start from the back of the church going in and out of each pew touching each parishioner. Father as you move through this church, blessing us*

17

with your holy spirit at the alter, we ask that you go left to right and right to left, touching each person from the crown of their head to the soles of their feet. We ask for a hedge of protection and a ring of fire around them. Whatever Father they stand in need of we ask that you granted it right now. Some are financial, health reasons, employment, housing, loneliness, children, spouses, family, drugs or trouble with the law. Whatever it is, Bless them Lord! And for those who are standing in the gap for a love one, please hear their pleas God and grant them their requests. Father we ask that you continue to bless the Shepherd of this house and his family. Continue to put your loving arms around him and continue to order his steps. Father we ask for traveling mercies to and from this house of worship. We ask that you continue to bless us minute by minute, hour by hour, and day by day. Father God you are a good God and we love you, and thank and praise your name! And Father what ever you do we already count it as blessed. These things we pray in your holy and precious name ! Amen. Let the Church say Amen." Say Amen again!

There was a lot of hugging, hallelujah's and rejoicing going on. This prayer was really felt by all. Sandra looked up and said thank you Lord, I sure needed that prayer. She looked at the boys and they were smiling and thanking God too!

After church Sandra and the boys went home. She said to herself I'm not going to let that Bill Collector ruin my life anymore; I'm going to trust in God. I'm going to stand up to him in a nice way and asked him to stop calling and harassing me.

Then I'm going to let God fight my battles. God said in his word, he'd make my enemies my footstool. And no weapon formed against me shall prosper! So I'm just going to wait on the Lord.

Sandra had a very good Sunday with no interruptions, knocks and phone calls. God had heard and answered her prayers. All day long Sandra was saying thank you Lord, thank you Lord!

Sandra took out her Bible and began reading the scriptures. She began to feel relieved. She knew everything was going to be alright. The joy of the Lord was her strength! Today was the first day in a long time that she didn't have a migraine headache or stomach ache.

While singing *"great is thy faithfulness"* she decided to cook her family a very nice delicious hot meal. After dinner still no calls from the Bill Collector. She looks up and gave thanks to God again. This is starting to feel good she said out loud.

"I'm free, hallelujah, thank God I'm free".

Sandra and the boys got out Alvin and the Chipmunk's Video to watch, and they popped some pop corn. She and the boys watched the video, ate pop corn and laughed all during the video. Sandra hadn't done this with her family in a long time. She really was at peace. Hmmm, she thought I need to get back to spending more family time with my family. The sermon this morning had been right on time for her.

MONDAY MORNING AT SANDRA'S HOUSE

EARLY MONDAY MORNING THE PHONE calls started coming in. She looked on the caller id and didn't answer the phone, while softly mumbling to her self; it's him again. Here we go again she said smiling to herself! Well at least I had one good day of rest. But Lord I'm ready for him now. She had her whole armor of God on! And now I know, I really know trouble don't last always. Before Sandra could get out of the house good, a loud knock comes on the door. Bam, bam, bam! He must have been sitting outside her house waiting to bust her.

Trippy whispers Nanny someone at the door. Then Trippy looks out the window and whispered Nanny it's the Bill Collector. Nanny whispers in Trippy's ear, and tells him to tell the Bill Collector that she's not home. Nanny runs and gets behind the door. Trippy opens the door and says Nanny said she's not home. The Bill Collector looks at Trippy and said "tell your mother the next time she goes out, to take her feet with her". The Bill collector saw Nanny's feet behind the door. Nanny and Trippy burst out laughing. What he said was so funny. This gave her a good laugh and some courage as well. Sandra felt like she was ready to take the Bill Collector on. Today she was ready to take on the world. Her confidence was finally back.

She shouted out loud . . . .

"No *weapon formed against me shall prosper and any evil tongue*
that rises up in judgment against me shall fall.!

Trippy looked puzzled. Nanny what you talking about?

The Bill Collector left with a big grin on his face and said I'll get
her yet, you just wait and see, he said under his breath. You just wait
and see. Just wait and see!

Later during the week he called again. Nanny answered and said
wrong number. He called right back and she said with an accent, no
speaky Englesh. This was really frustrating him. Now she trying to
sound like a foreigner. "He mumbled she thinks she's so smart. But if
it's the last thing I do, I will get her.

FRIDAY MORNING

EARLY ON FRIDAY MORNING SANDRA and her family saw the Bill Collector lurking around the house. He was looking through the window trying to peek in. She said it's on now. Sandra yelled out to Wayne and Michael to let Jade their "American Bull Dog" out of the house. Mike let Jade out through the the back door. Jade came slowly walking up behind the Bill Collector, drooling and sniffing at his butt. At first the Bill Collector didn't see Jade, but when he felt her breath, he turned around and saw Jade. His eyes got real big, he screamed, stumbled and fell over one of the bushes. Then he got up screaming and went running down the street. Jade is a 80 pound sweet lovable bull dog. All she does is lick and drool over you. But the Bill Collector didn't know that. After seeing Jade he ran so fast he forgot his car. He ran right past it. He was running do fast, that it looked like he was flying.

Sandra and her family were watching through the window. They laughed so hard that they fell to the floor crying and laughing hysterically.

This really made Sandra's day. She began singing "Oh Happy Day". "Oh Happy Day when Jesus Walked he washed my sins away".

Mom you're so funny said Michael. No Mikey she answered, God is good honey, God is so good, he's always right on time.!

This was the first time that Sandra had ever seen the Bill Collector in person. Hum she thought to herself he's not bad looking at all. As a matter of fact he is fine and built too! She though maybe I should try to meet him. He's put me through a lot and he needs to know it. She was really getting her courage and confidence back.

After all Sandra was a fine brick house herself. I can't wait until I tell Andrea and Brenda what he looked like. He sure is fine she repeated under her breath. He's who I'm been afraid of? This Bill Collector sure ain't what I expected. I was looking for a big ole burly ugly guy. His voice sure don't go with his looks. Sandra just stood in the floor in a daze. Thinking that she couldn't believe what she saw. Then she thought maybe he isn't the one. Maybe he's a substitute. Then she said now I'm confused.

She didn't want to ask the boys how he looked. Sandra didn't want them to know what she was thinking. She said under breath she would have Brenda look out for him. Now she really wanted to know if it was really him.

SANDRA'S HOUSE/FRIDAY NIGHT

TODAY WAS EVERYONE'S PAY DAY and tonight was the big house party. Everyone came with their own food and brown bags. The music was on and pumping loud and hard. The song "ain't nothing going on but the rent", was playing, then do the butt, momma popcorn, flashlight and song after song was played. What a party.

Someone shouted it's a party over here, party over here!

Then comes the knock again. It was loud and hard. He knocked so hard, that it sound like the door would come off the hinges!

"Bill Collector he shouted".

"I hear you in there he shouted, open the door, open the door right now"!

This made Sandra real mad. She just about had enough of his loud knocks.

Sandra told everyone to just ignore him, we gonna party tonight. Turn up the music and put on "Friday night just got paid" and let him knock.

The Bill Collector was frustrated when he heard that song. What nerve, she knows she has to pay this bill and she gonna put that record on. "Friday Night just got paid" on. Ooh just wait I'm gonna get her yet. He walks away, with his head hung low and feeling almost defeated.

Everyone was dancing and singing "It's Friday Night Just Got Paid", money in my pocket, booty shaking and we're dancing to the beat, partay, partay. Get down yawl, get down! John pulled out his whistle and began to blow it. Someone shouted, put your hands in the air just like you don't care. They were on fire. The party was on. The Bill Collector stood outside for a minute before leaving frustrated.

The gang partied hard all night. Everyone was in good spirits. Girl this party was slamming! We had a good time. Well it's time for you to go home. Okay Sandra, we're going. We're going, but we can't wait until next week. We sure had a good time tonight! Thanks Slim, I'm glad you did. Sandra's guest began to file out one by one.

Whew she said it was a good party tonight! I can't wait until I get in my bed tonight. I have completely worn myself out.

As Sandra was preparing for bed the phone rings again. She looks at her clock and wondered who the (LL) was calling her at 3:00 am. If it's that Bill collector I'm going to give him a piece of my mind she said out loud.

But when she looked at the caller Id, she saw that it was her girlfriend Andrea. Hello hey girl what's up? I know it's late but I've been calling you all night and the phone just kept ringing. Sorry but we were in here partying. The music was pumping so loud, that we didn't hear the phone ring. Girl we were trying to drown out the Bill Collector's knocks and calls. I wondered where you were. I forgot about the Friday night parties. Yeah girl we really "partayed" tonight. Andrea what's up?

Sandra I'm calling you because I want you to go with me to a wedding next Saturday. I know how you have been praying for God to

25

send you someone special in your life. If you come with me I'm sure you will find someone nice. There are going to be a lot of nice fine, single and wealthy men there. So you need to go with me! Andrea, Oh I don't know! I don't have any money or anything to wear. Girl we are the same size and I know you can find something to wear out of my closet.

Plus since I asked you to come as my guest I'll give the gift from the both of us. Sandra got silent and then said I don't know Andrea.

Sandra you know we are friends. And that just what friends do. Look out for one another.

Please Sandra please. Okay Andrea you don't have to beg me, I'll go with you. Andrea do you really have something for me to wear? I said I did. Sandra can you come over tomorrow afternoon. Then we can pick something out for you to wear. Yes I'll be there around 2:00 pm.

Sandra didn't sleep well that night. Because she kept dreaming about the Bill Collector. She woke up in a cold sweat. As she sat in bed, looking around, she asked herself what was wrong, why was she dreaming about him. After all the trouble he caused her, the headaches and stomach aches, now she had the nerve to be dreaming about him. Am I going crazy she asked herself. What is happening to me? She throws her hands up and screams, I can't take it anymore.

Sandra went downstairs and made herself a cup of hot chocolate. Her nerves were so frazzled. She finally fell asleep on the couch.

As usual one of the children came in to wake her up. But this morning she was already up moving about. She finally got a good night sleep on the couch. And her headache finally went away. Sandra went in the kitchen and fixed breakfast for her family.

Today, Sandra's sister Darlene was getting the boys and taking them to a church function. They would be gone all day. This would allow Sandra time to go to Andrea's house to find something to wear.

After the children left. Sandra took a hot shower and got ready to go to Andrea's. She put on a hot pink two piece short set with matching pink spiked heels. They really made her shapely legs look good. As usual her hair was tight, with every strand in place. Sandra was fine as wine and whatever she wore looked good on her. She really was a looker.

As Sandra leaves her house she looks around. This was a daily ritual for her. The coast was clear, there was no signs of the Bill Collector. She got into her car and headed over to Andrea's house.

The air was clear and the sun was out. Andrea rolled down the windows in her car so the cool breeze could hit her face. She had a convertible, but she hadn't gained enough confidence to just let the top down yet. She thought in due time, I'll be able be to let my convertible top down for the world to see me. Just as soon as I confront him I'll be completely free, and won't have to run and hide anymore. She shouted out loud. Thank you Lord, thank you!

ANDREA'S HOME

SANDRA RINGS THE BELL WHILE looking over her shoulders to make sure the Bill Collector hadn't followed her and was wasn't lurking around. She still had her guards up. Andrea open the door and they gave each other their usual girlfriend hug. Sandra I'm so glad you made it. Let's go into my bedroom closet, Sandra to see what we can find for you to wear.

Sandra walked into Andrea's bedroom and saw how huge her closet was. She jumped back saying, "Wow" this was the biggest clothes and shoe closet that she had ever seen. Now that's what I'm talking about she said. There was so much to chose from that she didn't know where to get started. Andrea had clothes and shoes galore. She had so many items of clothing and shoes still with tags on them. Andrea did have her closet very organized. She had her clothes grouped into their perspective categories. So it was very easy to find evening and dress wear for special occasions.

Andrea you must be shop-a-holic. You have so many clothes that you haven't even worn yet. Ah girl don't be silly. In time I'll wear them.

Sandra today we aren't here to talk about how many clothes I have, but we're here to find something for you to wear. We got to make sure you're right. You will be the bell of the wedding. All eyes will be focused on you!

Andrea what color will the bridal party be wearing?

Andrea replied they are wearing "Champagne colored gowns and accessories." So Sandra we don't want to clash with them. But of course we'll look as good as them or even better.

Sandra looks, and looks through racks and racks of clothes and finally saw a dress that she thought was the bomb. It looked like it was made for her. It was a peach colored spaghetti strap form fitting dress. It would accentuate her golden caramel color skin and her hazel colored eyes. This was the dress for her, plus Sandra had the figure for it too.

She would match it up with black three inch patent leather heels and a patent leather clutch. To touch it off she would accent it with a peach colored beaded necklace, bracelet and earrings set.

When Sandra tried the outfit on, she even whistled at herself. All she could say was wow. Tears started to form in her eye. She hadn't gotten dressed up like this in years. There was never any money to buy clothes or to go out. Everything she had extra went to the Bill Collector's bill.

Andrea came into the room and squealed with delight and said Sandra you look like a million dollars. If I were a man I would go out with you!

Okay Andrea this is what I want to wear. Sandra gave Andrea a big sisterly hug, said thanks and gather the outfit and told Andrea she would talk to her later.

Oh Andrea I almost for got. Forgot what Sandra. Girl I saw him. Who you talking about, Sandra? Andrea, the Bill Collector. What, when, where and how? When did you see him? Andrea he came to the house and Michael let Jade out the back door on him. Girl, Jade got behind him while he was looking in the window. When he finally saw Jade his eyes got so big, he fell over one of the bushes then he got up running. His hair was standing on top of his head. Girl he ran so fast, he ran past his car. We looked out the door and saw him two blocks away. He was so scared he left his car. We hollered, it was the funniest thing you ever saw.

We had tears in our eyes. That really made our day. I finally felt like we were getting him back for all his torture and harassment.

Oh girl, I think he must have come back late that night because his car was gone when we got up this morning. Sandra, well what did he look like? Girl he was fine as wine, and he looked like a Mandingo Warrior. He was tall, buffed and milk chocolate. He had dreamy green bedroom eyes with jet black wavy hair. He also had a very thin sexy mustache. After seeing him I felt a little different about him. He had such a terrified look on his face. That was really a Kodak moment! I almost feel sorry for him, because girl he has been trying for a very long time to catch me.

Now that I've seen him, he's someone that I would like to meet. I just don't know how. Ah girl don't be silly there will be many single guys to chose from at the wedding. Well established guys with beautiful homes, cars, money and their own businesses. Sandra don't give him a second thought!

Forget about him! Besides look how long he's been harassing you!

He had you on the verge of a nervous breakdown. Yeah I guess you're right.

Well I have to go. Luv you. Luv you too Sandra. And Sandra be careful going home. Keep your mind on the road and not on the Bill Collector. I'll be careful.

RIDING HOME

WHILE DRIVING HOME SANDRA THOUGH to herself "maybe my luck is changing". I know God must have heard my prayers. Because even though the Bill Collector has been harassing me, I kept wishing for a good man to come into my life for me and my boys; and to love us. And now I might just find him. Then she said out loud, Lord I sure hope, I find Mister Wright at the wedding. Tears were rolling down her face. Then she looked in the rear view mirror and thought this is the best thing that has happened to me in a long time.

"I haven't been out formally in a very long time. And, just think my best friend is taking me somewhere nice; where I may be able to find the man of my dreams. Wow she exclaimed! God must have heard my prayers. Every night before I go to sleep I pray that God would send me someone to share my life with. But not just any man! He would have to accept my children, be a working man, love the Lord, attend church, be "kinda" good looking with a nice body but most of all, a man that would love me for me! I guess I drew the right picture this time! All my doodling has finally paid off.

While looking again in her rear view mirror she said "no I am not asking for too much or being too particular". Because the Bible says:

"Ask for what you want and he'll give you the desires of your heart", Amen! She looks up to the heavens with a smile on her face and says, Thank you God!

Just as Sandra was driving up to her house she looked again in her rear view mirror, and a picture of the Bill Collector appeared. Oh my God it's him. She pulled over to avoid having an accident. When she looked one more time his face had disappeared. Sweat started pouring down her face as she sat in her car violently shaking. After sitting in her car for about five minutes she said out loud to herself, I need to stop being so silly, my mind is starting to play tricks on me. Oh well she thought he's just a Bill Collector. I just need to forget him. Sandra walks into her house.

As she enters her home Sandra shouts in a very excited voice, family come here. They all came running out, asking her what was wrong. Mom is everything alright. Sandra holds up her bags and says I'm going out with Aunt Andrea and she letting me wear theses things. I'm going to look fabulous.

Ah Mom you're already fabulous, said Anthony and Michael. Mom you really scared us, when you screamed we thought something bad had happened to you. "Let me see the dress Nanny", Trippy said while tugging at her bags.

Sandra took out the dress and the accessories so that her family could see them. Then she waltzed off to her bedroom. She was smiling, while her heart was pounding with joy. The boys were so happy for their Mom and Nanny. They hated to see her upset. This was a good thing.

She couldn't wait to get to work to share her good news with her co-workers. They always had some good advise for her. Some of her co-workers had been trying for a while to get Sandra to go out to the club with them. But you know the fear of the Bill Collector kept her a prisoner at home. They kept telling her that she wasn't living, and that she was only existing.

WORK

ON MONDAY MORNING SANDRA COULDN'T wait to get to work to share her good news with her co-workers. Good morning everyone! Her co-workers looked surprise. Because Sandra was dancing and singing. Her other friend Brenda said good morning, Sandra you sure are chipper. I am "yawl" gather around so that I can share my good news with you!

I'm going out this weekend to a wedding. I have the most gorgeous dress and shoes to wear. And yawl, Andrea said there will be plenty of single, handsome and wealthy men at the wedding. She chirped, as she began to dance around, right now I am in heaven and I'll be so pretty, so very pretty! Everyone started laughing. Girl you're so crazy.

After sharing her news they all offered her some tips on how to act while she was out. You see her co-workers were some of the same ones who attended her Friday night house parties.

Sandra make sure you get phone numbers and don't give up too much information about yourself. And make sure you bring a camera, so that you can take pictures to look at when you get home. And of course we want to see them too. So don't forget to bring them in to work. Yeah don't forget said Brenda. As the week wound down Sandra was getting more and more anxious and excited. She couldn't wait to attend the wedding with Andrea. Sandra hadn't been this excited in years. And all she was doing, was going to a wedding.

All of a sudden a sadness started to over take her. In spite of all of her excitement this week, something felt very strange. Monday, Tuesday, Wednesday, Thursday and today Friday, no calls or visits from the Bill Collector. She wondered what was wrong. Oh well she thought maybe he decided to leave me alone. She had kind of gotten used to his calls and knocks at her door. Since he's decided to leave me alone, I can get on with my life she thought. Maybe Jade really scared him she thought. He really was funny running down the street. He gave us a good laugh.

Wow my luck surely has changed. Sandra sent a shout up to God.

Thank you Lord, thank you.

But Something still was missing. What is it? She couldn't shake the way she was feeling. It's Friday she repeated again, and the Bill Collector still hadn't called her or even snooped around her house. That is very strange. This made her feel kind of sad. Sandra had grown accustomed to his calls even though they were harassing. Maybe he's sick or out of town. Hmmm. She wondered or was she just a gluten for punishment?

Hmmm let me call Brenda to see if she's seen him around. Before Sandra could make her call, her phone rang first. Oh my, I must have spoken too soon she thought. As she went to pick up the phone she saw on the caller id that it was Brenda. Whew she said. Hello, hello Brenda what's up. You were on my mind. I was getting ready to call you, and then you rang the phone.

Brenda have you seen the Bill Collector around in the neighborhood?

No one had seen or heard from him. Girl a week is too long for him not bother us. He has been very persistent for months. Now we don't hear anything from him. And even though he was a pest I'm a little worried. Sandra didn't you want him to stop bothering you?

Yeah. Then count it as a blessing. Count it all joy! I guess you're right she replied in a low sad voice. Then Sandra said out loud now I know God has heard my prayers no more Bill Collector. Sandra you better watch what you ask for, because you just might get it. I guess you right Brenda.

Brenda I guess this calls for a small celebration. Brenda round up the gang. Sandra that's what I been waiting to hear!

Everything will be ready when you get off tonight. And Sandra since you're going out tomorrow we can have the party at my house. This way you won't have to spend your time cleaning up. You can get rest and be ready for your affair. Sounds good to me Brenda. Girl I luv you. You're the best friend a girl could ask for. Brenda since I'm going out tomorrow I will only be at the party for a little while.

FRIDAY NIGHT

SANDRA COMES HOME FROM WORK and get cleaned up so that she can go next door to the party. Ring, ring hi Sandra the gang is all here. The party was in full swing. The dance floor was packed everybody was shaking their booties.

Kool and the Gang was playing *"get down get down"*, Sandra eased her way into the kitchen, and asked Brenda had she seen the Bill Collector yet. Brenda threw her hands up. Sandra I thought you were going to forget him. I know she replied, but you know he always comes knocking on Friday nights. Something is wrong. I can feel it. I wonder if he's sick. Sandra was still remembering the glimpse she got of him. Even though she didn't know him, she was starting to think about him more and more.

Oh well I've got more important things to think about., and that's my day at the wedding tomorrow with Andrea.

Saturday finally comes. Sandra wakes up bright and early. She set her hair and did her nails. Later she went down and had fruit, juice and toast for breakfast. I don't want to eat too much I know there will be plenty of food to eat at the reception.

The kids were staying at her grandmother's for the weekend. That's one thing she didn't have to worry about. Sandra's grandmother would be over to get them before Sandra left to go out. Her grandmother wanted to make sure her makeup and hair was right and that she had everything else in place.

After breakfast she had a couple of hours before she needed to get ready. I'll take a beauty nap she whispered to herself. As Sandra slept she began to dream about the Bill Collector. He was chasing her through a field of lilies. And as she was running and laughing while looking back saying "you'll never catch me", then the Bill Collector began running faster and faster after her. And just as he was about to catch hold of Sandra, she woke up! I must have been dreaming she said smiling as she stretched her arms over her heads.

Hum she thought why am I dreaming about him. What does this mean? Oh well I don't know, but it's time for my shower. The shower was nice and hot and the steam made a figure on the glass door. It was his face, "The Bill Collector"; I must be dreaming she thought. Lord what is happening to me? Am I going crazy. What's wrong with me she kept asking herself?

Sandra gets out of the shower and dries off while trying to put him out of her mind. She said down and began to shake. What is happening to me? I'm suppose to be happy, but I just can't forget his face.

Brenda calls just in the nick of time, to ask if she needed help getting dress. And of course Brenda had to see what Sandra had been raving about all week. Come on over girl and please help me to get dressed. I'll be right over.

Sandra put her make on and Brenda help her to get dressed. Brenda I have to tell you something. I hope you don't think I'm crazy but I keep dreaming about the Bill Collector. I see his face everywhere in my dreams. You know just a few minutes ago his face appeared on my shower door. This last week has been crazy. Brenda what does it mean? Girl I don't know, but it sounds spooky to me. Woo, woo said Brenda. Ah girl, stop it. I' m just being funny, Sandra I don't know what means.

Sandra is finally all dressed with her accessories on. Girl you look like a million dollars Brenda said. The poor bride ain't going to stand a chance with you around. Sandra all eyes are going to be on you. If you don't find a man today something is terrible wrong. If I were a man I would go out with you myself. You're looked so beautiful sweetie and your smile could light up a city. Sandra and you need to put the Bill Collector out of your mind. Today is your day to have some real fun.

Thanks Brenda I needed that. Wish me luck she said. When Sandra came downstairs her children said Mom is that you? You look slamming. Mom you look fabulous. Mom let us take your picture.

Just as they finished posing a knocks comes on the door. Sandra jumps. She thinks maybe she spoke too soon. Trippy runs to the door and looks out. It's Grand mom. Whew, I thought it was him she said.

As Mrs. Elaine McCallum enters her home and get a glimpse of Sandra she stops in her track while grasping her chest. Wow Sandra you look amazing. You just took my breath away. Well granddaughter you said you wanted to find someone nice. If you don't catch someone's eye, today something is really wrong. Because baby you look stunning. That dress was really made for you. You are really wearing it too!

Sandra and her grandmother posed for her children. Then Brenda took pictures of the whole family. Sandra make sure you have, your camera, cell phone and some money with you. And of course make sure you have a great time!

She was finally off to meet Andrea at her house. It seemed liked it took forever to get to Andrea's house. Finally she arrives there. Her nerves were causing her to start to worry. I can't wait to get to Andrea. I have taken this ride so many times and it never seemed this long before, she said.

Ring, ring, coming Andrea shouted. When she opened the door, Andrea's mouth flew opened. Sandra you look stunning. That dress looks better on you then it does on me. Girl you really are wearing that dress, so it's yours to keep! Andrea do you really mean I can have this dress. Of course I do, Sandra. It has your name on it! This act of kindness filled Sandra up. It had been a long time since anyone had really showed her such a nice act of kindness. Yeah she had her friends from the Friday Night House Parties. But this was something special for her; and to be treated like a Queen was what she needed. Tears started to fall, and Andrea rushed and gave her a tissue and said "now wipe your eyes".

"Sandra you don't want to mess up your makeup and girl you deserve this and more. You just wait your day is coming real soon", trust me Sandra, it's coming real soon!

Andrea asked Sandra if she was ready. You bet Andrea yes I'm ready. We'll ride in my car, Sandra. Andrea had a black 500 Mercedes Benz sports car. Sandra said this is too good to be true, heaven must have sent you from above.

As they rode along, Sandra was basking in how good she looked. They finally arrived at their destination. The wedding was being held in the sprawling gardens of the L. Johnson's Mansion. The property was two miles long. They were greeted at the entrance by a valet, who took their car to park. A luxurious trolley was waiting to ride them up to the wedding site. Sandra was so amazed that she actually was in a place like that. All she could do was stare with her mouth wide open.

Close your mouth child and do what I do. They walked inside and were greeted by attendants who directed them to the gardens where the wedding would be held. The house was massive and very beautiful. The huge spiraling stair case and marble floors was to die for. The White Baby Grand Piano which sat in the middle of the room really set the room off. There were flowers everywhere. A violinist was in the atrium playing until the wedding began. Andrea saw a few of her friends out in the garden. She blew kisses to acknowledge that she saw them. The day was so perfect with bright sunshine and a little breeze. Hundreds of White Doves were circling overhead in the beautiful floral gardens.

WEDDING CEREMONY

As THE GROOM AND THE pastor approach the podium the music began to play. The soloist sang the Lord's prayer. She had a beautiful melodious voice which stirred up the audience. Then the processional began with the ring bearer entering first. He was a cute three year old ring bearer who came running down the aisle. Next came the three flower girls. The two small flower girls dropped rose petals. They were so cute. An the older flower girl gave out chocolate kisses to every person at the end of each pew.

Sandra whispered to Andrea how cute they were. After the bridal party entered on Endless Love. It was time to stand, because the Bride and her father were entering on Isn't she lovely by Stevie Wonders. The bride was simply gorgeous. Sandra had an opportunity to sneak a peek and look the audience over. There were so many gorgeous single men in the crowd. This was very unusual because at most weddings the women usually out number the men. I hope they're all straight she said under her breath. Andrea hit her lightly on her arm and said stop it girl, just wait and see!

The wedding ceremony was so beautiful. The couple added their own special touches to the ceremony. After the ceremony was over the people filed out of the gardens into the area for the reception. A band played dance music, while the waiters came around with scrumptious bites to eat; mini crab cakes, shrimp, quiches, chocolate covered strawberries, chicken bites and all kinds of cheese and fruits. There was so much to choose from. And of course the champagne was flowing. Sandra told Andrea she could get full off of the appetizers, but she was trying to wait for the main course. Yeah girls these appetizers are slamming she replied.

As Sandra continue to look around the gardens, one guy caught her eye. He looked familiar to Sandra. But she couldn't quite put her hands on where she knew him. She asked Andrea had she seen him before. Andrea had no idea who he was. From time to time Sandra saw him watching her. But she played it off. There also were other guys looking at Sandra but she had her eyes on the guy who had been watching her.

The Head waiter came around and announced that everyone should take their seats at the dinner tables. Everyone took their seats for dinner. The tables were done up so beautifully, with beautiful floral arrangements.

For dinner they served lobster tail, filet minion and lemon chicken smother in wine sauce. Along with the meats were sautéed broccoli, asparagus, baby green peas, and wild rice pilaf with shallots and mushrooms. The waiters had to bring more hot buttered rolls to most of the tables. The guest were eating them before the dinner was served.

The meal was hot and delicious and the service was top notch. They left no stones untouched.

The bride requested banana pudding for desert. She gave them special instructions on how to prepare it. The caterer got it right. Everyone commented on how good it tasted. Sandra said it almost tasted as good as her son's Mikey's Banana's Pudding!

Finally the party started and everyone was on the dance floor dancing to the electric slide, sugar hill etc. This was her kind of party. Sandra loved to dance. But she hadn't been out dancing in years. That's why they had the house parties. Sandra and Andrea were on the floor doing the electric slide dance. It seemed like all eyes were on them. Andrea was looking good herself. She too had a slamming body. Andrea had on a lime green form fitting dress that complimented Sandra's dress. They both were knockouts.

Finally the wedding coordinator announced that the bride would be throwing the bouquet and the groom would throw the garter.

All single women please come to the floor, she said.

Sandra said she wasn't getting up there. Andrea convinced her to get up there, saying she would go up with her. Finally she said okay. They both went up hoping to catch the bouquet. Wouldn't you know it Sandra caught the bouquet. I can't believe it, she said while holding the bouquet to her heart. This must be my lucky day! Everything is coming up roses for me, she whispered under breath.

Then it was time for the men. Half of the room came up. One, two, three. Guess who caught it. The guy that had been looking at her all afternoon. This really must be my day she said. Me, then him! Wow!

The guy who caught the garter was thinking the same thing that Sandra was thinking. I know her from somewhere, but where he thought.

But I'm glad she's the one that caught the bouquet. I have been wanting to talk to her ever since I saw her. This must be my lucky day he thought!

The coordinator called them both up. As Sandra sat down in the chair they both gazed into each others eyes.

Mmmm, He was a tall milk chocolate, built handsome hunk, with gorgeous green colored eyes she said under her breath. And she was fine as wine he mumbled to himself. It was now time for the man to put the garter on the woman. As he bent down on his knee she got a closer look. Damm that man is fine and he smells good too she thought. He said the same thing about her under his breath.

Sandra made sure she smelled good herself. She had her far away perfume on. He has her leg and began to push the garter up her leg.

(nice legs he said under his breath)

Whoa she said not to far. He looked at her and smiled. Hold it, shouted the photographer, let me take a picture. The photographer walked over to the couple and said looked at the camera, but keep your hand on her leg. He was loving this because he was able to hold on to her leg a little while longer. One, two, ready smile. Click it was done. Okay I'm finished the photographer told them. As she got up from the chair he looked at Sandra and said what is your name? Michelle she replied. That was her middle name, she didn't really want to lie to him. So what's your name, she asked. Brian he replied. They both asked in unison are you with someone. No he said. Well I'm here with my girlfriend Andrea. As a matter of fact, that's her sitting over there. She's the reason that I'm here. She invited me as her guest! I'm so glad that she invited you.

He turned and said do you want to dance. Yes I would love to. They danced through four songs. Then Sandra remembered that Andrea was sitting alone. I have to go to see about my friend. He followed her to the table and Sandra introduced him to Andrea. Hello Andrea, I'm Brian, nice to meet you! Andrea I want to thank you for bringing Michelle with you. He winked at Sandra and said I'll talk with you later.

Sandra sat down she had to catch her breath. Andrea grabbed Sandra's hand and said girl he is fine, I mean skin bone fine. You better not let him get away. I know Andrea but I feel like I know him from somewhere, but I can't figure out where. Sandra he called you Michelle. What's that all about. Andrea, Michelle is my middle name, and I still think I know him from somewhere so before I get to know him I don't want to give my first name up yet. I got you, girl. I know that's right, Andrea replied.

After the bride and groom cut the cake they decided to leave. Sandra was having so much fun that she forgot she had the camera for pictures. Brian came over and asked if he could see her again. This was her chance to get a picture. Brian can I take your picture she asked. Oh let me take a picture of both of you Andrea said. Okay Andrea; Brian do you mind? No Sandra I would love to take a picture with you.

May I have your phone number, he asked. Sandra smiled at him and decided to give him her cell phone number. He took her hand and kissed it and said you'll be hearing from me real soon. Brian gave her a wink and walked away. She so was memorized while saying this was must be heaven. She looks up and said "Thank you Lord, Thank you"

As they rode home Sandra couldn't thank Andrea enough. This has been one of the best days in my life. I had a wonderful time. Thank you Andrea. Oh you don't have to thank me, I'm glad that you had a good time. I did Andrea, I did she said. Girl I love you for inviting me out! Sandra this was your day, I did this for you. You deserve to be happy. And like I told you, that what's friends are for! Sandra hugs Andrea with tears in her eyes and thanked her for her friendship and giving ways. Andrea I love you! Sandra I love you too! That's what real friends do. We need to help one another.

I just hope he pans out, and that he is who you've been waiting for. And Sandra he's a lucky guys, because there were so many guys who had their eyes on you all night. A couple of them came to me while you were dancing trying your get your name and phone number. Girl you were wearing that dress. You really were!

Later that night Sandra got a call. Hello, Michelle, this is Brian. I've been thinking about you ever since you left. I hope it's alright for me to call. Oh sure, it's alright. She didn't want to let him know how anxiously she was wanting to hear from him so she had to play it cool. For a minute she thought he wouldn't call and that he was just another pretty face!

After a minute of silence, Sandra said it was a beautiful wedding wasn't it Brian? Yes Michelle everything was just beautiful. And the couple really looked in loved with each other.

Then Brian said, Michelle what are you doing next Saturday evening? Nothing right now. Well Michelle I have tickets to the ***Bozys to Men Concert*** and I want to know if you will be my date. I would love too she replied. I can pick you up at 6:00 pm. Let me know where. Sandra still was being cautious. She didn't want him just yet to know where she lived. So she told him to pick her up at Andrea's house.

After they hung up Sandra called Andrea and told her what she had done. No problem girl you know we have to look out for one another.

You can use my house. All week long Sandra was a nervous wreak. Something still kept nagging at her. I feel like I know him. But I can't put my finger on where I know him from. She racked her brain but nothing came up.

Sandra told her neighbor Brenda that she had met a very nice and fine guy. But girl I feel like I already know him. What does he look like Brenda asked? After describing him, Brenda scratched her head and said he sound like the Bill Collector to me. Don't you remember that's how you described him to me. Don't you remember Sandra what he looks like? You know Brenda I thought I got a good look at him the last time he came around. Sandra what if it is him? I don't know she said. And now I kinda like him. He seems like he like me too. I don't think he knows who I am. He's never seen me. Well anyway, Andrea is letting me use her house and he will pick me up there.

I'm just going to play it by ear. Sandra just be careful. I will she replied.

Saturday finally rolls around. Sandra went to Andrea's house early so she could wait for Brian. Andrea, girl I think he might be the Bill Collector. Are you sure? No I'm not really positive but he sure looks like him. Sandra just be careful. I need to get the pictures developed so that I can analyze the pictures. Do you have your cell phone with you. Yeah girl I keep it with me at all times. Well if you need me just call. I'll be right there. Sandra I will be waiting up for you to get back in, it doesn't matter what time you get in.

She embraces Andrea and said thanks girls I love you. Just as she walked away from Andrea the door bell rang. Ring, ring, ring Sandra comes to door and looks through the peep hold. It's him she said. Andrea went into the kitchen so he wouldn't see her. She opens the door and lets him in. Hi Michelle he said and reaches over and kisses her on the cheek. You look very nice and smells good too he said. She was wearing a two piece white linen pants suit. He handed her a single yellow rose and said this is for you. Oh Brian that so special. She laid it on the table in the foyer. You're special he replied.

Brian had a bright shiny black Jaguar waiting for them. He touch her hand as they rode away to the show. A warm feeling came over her. Then all of a sudden she started to get butterflies in her stomach. She hadn't felt like this in along time. What could this be she thought. From time to time she felt Brian looking at her. She was afraid to look back fearing that he might see her looking.

Finally they arrived at the theater. There were so many people there.

Excitement started to well up inside of her as they approach their seats. Wow they had very good seats, three rows from the front. Brian didn't tell her that he was a cousin to one of the guys in the ***Bozys to Men group***.

The show was awesome. ***Bozys to Men***, really threw down, they had the crowd on their feet almost throughout the whole show. The group opened up with ***Song for Momma***, and they continued singing ***Growing Up***, ***End of the Road***, ***Four Seasons of Love***, ***I Miss You***, ***Water Runs Dry***, ***Amazing***, ***The color of love***, ***The Perfect Love Song*** and they closed with ***I'll make love to you***. This was such a treat for her. She always wanted to attend their concert but could never afford to attend one. Brian also surprised Sandra after the show by taking her to meet the group in their dressing room. You see—Shaun Stockman was Brian's first cousin. They had not seen each other in a very long time. Sandra was really siked and surprised at the same time. Seeing a BOZY To Men Concert, and then actually meeting them was awesome! This really blew her mind. All Sandra kept saying was wow, wow! Brian never told her that Shaun was his cousin. What a double treat this was for her. Seeing the show then actually getting the opportunity to meet the group up front.

Once they left the arena Brian took Sandra to a little after hours jazz club. It was small but quaint and intimate. Brian ordered some buffalo wings and wine. The wine made Sandra relax some. They began talking trying to get to know each other. Every now and then, Sandra would try and peek at Brian when he was not looking at her. This was almost difficult for her to do, because Brian was looking at her like she was a piece of chocolate candy!

Sandra Michelle asked Brian what he did for a living. Oh I work for a large collection agency he replied. He told her a month ago he was promoted to senior district manager. Brian said he used to go out and try to collect monies owed from debtors. Michelle it's not an easy job, you hear all kinds of crazy stories why people don't pay. I feel sorry for some of the people, he said. But the ones that get my goat are the ones who try to get over. Michelle they do all kinds of things trying to avoid paying their debt. They make up all kinds stories just to avoid paying their bills. It can be very frustrating at times. And you know Michelle there is one Lady who even gets her children involved when I come to her house. This lady even let her dog out on me. I can't wait until I get her. She is the only case that I am still pursuing. She really thinks she smart, but I got something for her.

As he continue to talk a sinking feeling started coming over Sandra. It is him she thought! But how could this be. He seemed so nice and different tonight! The jaguar is what really threw her off. Because he always came to her house in the old beat up car when he was trying to get a payment. She was still hoping that it wasn't him, but her suspicions were being confirmed. It was him! Brian went on to say now all I do is supervise, a staff of collectors, do paper work, do the schedules, payroll and hold seminars. Michelle I decided to keep that one pesky case. I will keep this case until I nail her. She thinks she is so slick. But I'll get her, and it's going to be sooner than she thinks. Now when I call her house, my number comes up private so she won't know who's calling. Sandra said under her breath so that's who the private person is. She was kind of hip to it anyway, and wouldn't answer the private calls. Then she started to get worried. She had to think of something real fast to do.

Michelle thought to herself what if he finds me out. Should I tell him or wait and see. All of a sudden Michelle began to shake uncontrollably.

What's wrong honey, he asked. It might be the wine. I haven't had wine in a very long time. I just got over a cold and I think this cold is trying to come back she said. Brian you know sometimes me and wine don't get along. Michelle do you want me to take you home. Yes she replied, but first let me go to the ladies room.

Once inside the ladies room, the tearing started to flow. What am I going to do now she asked herself while wringing her hands? What am I going to do? I knew this was too good to be true she whimpered. After she wiped her eyes and gained her composure she walked out to him. Are you alright he asked. Oh I'm still feeling a little woozy and I need to go home and rest. She knew this was the only way that she didn't have to talk about herself to him. Brian I hope I didn't ruin your evening she said. Oh no Sandra I had a great time just being with you.

I hope that this will be a starts of a long lasting relationship and many more dates.

As they walked to the car, Sandra Michelle's mind was bursting with all kinds of thoughts. Brian was such a gentleman. He opened the door and helped her in the car. As they drove to her home, she thought I will fake being sleep so that I don't have to talk. She closed her eyes and laid her head on his shoulder. Brian looked and her and said my baby has gone to sleep. He turned the radio on and *"Just one life time"* was playing. This was one of Sandra's favorite songs. But she kept her eyes closed and listened. She wanted him to think that she was sleep. Brian sang along to the songs as they rode home.

She though he even has a beautiful voice. He can sing to me anytime. "Just one life of loving you honey won't be long enough, he sang". Sandra always sang this song. She always told her friends, once she learned this song, would be the day she would find true love! She wondered could he be the one.

BACK AT ANDREA'S

THEY FINALLY ARRIVED AT HER place. Brian reached over and gently shook her and said wake up sleepy head. She whimpered and looked lost for a minute. He said we're at your house. She sat up rubbing her eyes. Then Sandra gazed into Brian eyes and said, was I sleep. Yes honey I guess it was the wine. He walked her to the door and gave her a small but gentle kiss on her lips. Brian thank you so much I had a wonderful time. He said so did I. When can I see you again? She smiled and said call me. Then he took Sandra's hands and said Michelle I really like you. He pulled her close and gave her kiss on her cheek. He looked at her and said please feel better. Sandra went inside Andrea's house as fast as she could.

By the time Sandra got inside she was hyperventilating and gasping for air. She was so glad that Andrea was still up. Andrea came running and asked her what was wrong. I think he knows who I am. Andrea he is the Bill Collector. I knew it, I knew it was him. How do you know it is him? I know it's him. When we shared with each other, he said that he collected outstanding debts and that their was one lady that he's been trying to get for a long time. Ah girl you're just being paranoid. No Andrea, he said I let Jade out on him. He said he's going to get me. Just wait and see what happens. Then she began crying uncontrollably.

Hush up now. We'll think of something. It's going to be alright.

Girl stay in my spare bedroom tonight and get some sleep. You need to calm your nerves! You're in no condition to drive home tonight. Thanks Andrea you're my Angel!

Brian called Sandra about an hour later to see how she was feeling. In her sleepy voice she said just a little better. Okay baby go back to sleep and I will call you tomorrow. Goodnight she whispered to him. She was so glad that he didn't insist on talking.

She tossed and turned all night, wondering what she was going to do. Her feelings were really out there and she didn't want to lose him.

Finally she meets someone that she likes and in a twinkling of an eye it could be lost. Finally Sandra gets out of beds and get on her knees and begins to pray.

> *"Father God I come to you one more time, me your daughter Sandra.*
> *Father I need help in this situation. You finally sent me someone*
> *that I could love and now I might lose him. Father please send me a*
> *message on what I need to do. Father please hurry.*
> *Thank you, Lord, amen!*

Sandra got back in bed. Finally a peace came over her and she was able to fall asleep.

WEEKLY PHONE TALKS

BRIAN STARTED CALLING MICHELL EVERYDAY. Sometimes they would talk 3 to 4 times a day. Brian was growing on her real fast. She liked him a lot. And he like her too. It was something very special about him that she liked.

Maybe he doesn't know it's me after all she thought.

On the following Monday a knock came at the door, Bill Collector he called out. Sandra recognized the voice. That's him. I thought he said he didn't do this anymore. Then she remembered that he said this the only case that he would pursue. So I guess he really wants to get me. Trippy come here. Hurry up come here. What Nanny ? Go to the door and tell the Bill Collector I'm not at home. Trippy went to the door and cracked it a little bit and said my Nanny said she's not home. The Bill Collector told Trippy to tell her to call the office when she got home.

Sandra looked out of the window and watched him walk away. It was him, it really was him. She cried out.

Now what am I going to do. Should I tell him I need some help.

Brian called all week. But Sandra refuses to answer any of his phone calls. He wondered what was wrong. Maybe she doesn't like me, he thought. The Bill Collector even went to where he thought she lived

(Andrea's house). No one was there. I guess if she wants to talk she'll call me he said. But what did I do wrong he wondered. I thought she really like me. The Bill Collector had also fallen very hard for Sandra. He was really missing her too.

Finally one day Brian sees Sandra Michelle's out in the yard working her garden. She can't run or hide. As he walks towards her, she begins to shake and the tears started to flow like the River Niger. She stands there wondering what he would say to her. Brian walks up to her and says so you are the one that I've trying to collect a debt from all of this time.

Brian looks at her hard and said don't know what to say, huh. I'm mad at you but at the same time I've come to care about you. Michelle I have very strong feelings for you. Why didn't you tell me, he asked? I feel like a fool because all of this time I've been chasing you for a bill. And when I met you I would never have thought that I had found someone with a connection to me. Because you see we are connected in a strange way. This outstanding bill that you owe has us connected.

He looks at Sandra again and just walks away steaming. Sandra cries out don't go, please don't go. He kept walking shaking his head in disgust.

Brian gets in his (hoopty) car and drives away. He said I feel like a fool. She really betrayed me. He threw his hands up. What am I going to do? I like her. I really like her. Brian was so upset that he had to pull over to compose himself. Tears had welled up in his eyes. He had not felt this way about another woman in a very long time.

Sandra falls to the ground weeping uncontrollably. She stayed there for so long that it began to get dark. Brenda comes up on Sandra and asks what was wrong. Get up and come inside. Girl we need to talk. Sandra was still on the ground. He found me at home today and he really know its me she wails. Brenda he was here. He left and wouldn't come back. Calm down Sandra, what and who are you talking about? The Bill Collector who is my Brian. Yeah Brenda I couldn't get away.

He was here before I had a chance to do anything. She cried I've lost him I've lost the man of my dreams.

Sandra get up so we have to figure something out. You need to wipe your face. Your eyes are so swollen from crying, honey. Brenda walks Sandra into her house. Sandra was so distraught that she had to go to bed.

Get some rest sweety and I'll call you in the morning. Brenda kisses Sandra's forehead telling her everything will be alright.

This situation has really gotten her down. It was a good thing the kids were at her grandmothers' she didn't have the strength to talk about it with any one. This episode had taken so much out of her that all she wanted to do was sleep. Sandra cried herself to sleep.

NEXT MORNING

RING, RING, RING, SANDRA LOOKS at her caller ID to see who was calling. It was Brenda, Sandra didn't feel like talking so she rolled over and went back to sleep.

Brian couldn't get Sandra out of his mind either. He was really feeling her too. He began calling Sandra. He needed to talk and get some answers. Every five minutes he would call. Since he had her cell phone and house numbers, he called them both. He was determined to talk with her. Sandra didn't want to talk with anyone.

The kids were finally back home. Her grandmother called out to Sandra to let her know they were in the house. Okay Mom, she replied. I have a slight headache, so I won't be coming downstairs. She didn't want to have to answer her grandmothers' questions. Grand mom could be relentless at times. She didn't take no junk.

The phone rings again, and Trippy answers it. Nanny not home he said. Who are you he asked ? I'm Trippy her grandson! Sandra had schooled all the children that if anyone calls not to let them know she was there. And Trippy had recognized the Bill Collector voice because he had called so many times.

Then Trippy hangs the phone up. He runs in to the bedroom. Nanny, Nanny, Nanny! What Trippy?

Nanny the Bill Collector called and he wanted to know who I was. Nanny I told him I was your grandson. Nanny replied you did good Trippy, you did good. I don't want to talk to him now Trippy. Nanny please turn the ringer off. No baby leave it on. Trippy gets in the bed and gives Nanny a big kiss. Nanny I love you. I love you too Trippy. You know what Trippy I'm going to get up and the next time he calls, give the phone to me. Okay Nanny I will. Trippy runs off to wait for the phone to ring again.

LATE AFTERNOON

BRIAN CALLS SANDRA ON HER cell phone. She answers. Hello, Hi how are you Michelle? I'm alright Brian. How are you? I'm fine and a little confused he replied. Michelle I didn't think you were still talking to me. I wasn't at first. But Michelle I got just had to get over the initial shock. I bet you knew all the time who I was. I felt like you led me on.

Michelle?

Didn't you? Didn't you . . .

But, but Brian you never asked me. And I didn't really find out who you were until we were out on the dance floor at the club and you told me about your job, and then I didn't know how to tell you. I got scared and didn't know what to do. When we first went out I had a feeling that I knew you. Then I realized that it was really you when we danced together at the club.

Brian I didn't know what to do. I was hoping that you wouldn't find me out. I was trying to come up with a way of telling you. But you found me out before I could come up with someway to tell way.

Then Sandra started to cry uncontrollable.

Brian told her to stop crying. It's going to be alright. We will work something out he said. She finally pulled herself together.

Tears started to come again. Brian I'm sorry, so sorry.

Michelle why didn't you try and get some help. I did but the guy before you didn't want to hear anything. And Brian I was mad because it was my ex-husband's bill, and then I really didn't have the money to pay it. Brian all of my money goes to raising my children and Trippy. I don't even get my child support. I got tired of fighting for support. So you see there was never any extra money to pay this bill.

Michelle I'm going to see what I can do to get this bill erased. This bill is messing up your credit so we need to fix it. Plus it's ten years old. Our company has a debt consolidation plan. We also have a plan that will dissolve the debt if the debtor can't pay it because of extenuating circumstances.

And Brian since we are getting everything out in the open, I need to tell you that Michelle is my middle name. My first name is Sandra, I wanted to throw you off just in case it was really you. Michelle, Sandra do you have any more secrets that I need to know. Yes Brian the house that you picked me up at is my best friend Andrea's house. You met her at the wedding. And I have three sons and a grandson, Michael, Wayne, Anthony and Trippy my grandson. But the most important thing is that I started falling for you! I really like you.

Me too Michelle I'm falling for you. I guess it's time to get to know you and your family. Oh by the way I met your grandson Trippy on the phone. I think he's the one who comes to the door saying you aren't home. Michelle I had to laugh myself because I saw your feet behind the door, one of the times time I came to your house. Those were your feet, weren't they? This brought a big smile on Michelle's face. Yes Brian they were mine.

Michelle I have one question, do you prefer to be called Michelle or Sandra? Well everyone know me by Sandra. But I like the way you call me Michelle. So let me call you Sandra Michelle.

Brian I want to invite you over for dinner on Sunday to meet my family and close friends. Is five's clock good for you Brian? It's perfect! Do you need me to bring anything. No Brian just bring yourself. I have to hang up but I will be talking to you before Sunday. Sandra screams out loud. Yes! Thank you God, Thank you God for hearing my prayers! The Boys came running. Mom, Nanny you alright. Yes my loves everything is alright.

She said I gatta makes some calls. First I'll call Andrea since she was with me when we first met in person. Then I'll call Brenda. I want both of them at the dinner. Ring, ring, hello, hello. Andrea you'll never guess who's coming to dinner. Who Sandra? Brian the Bill Collector. What, how did you manage that. Well we finally talked. Trippy answered the phone and told him that I wasn't home. I think he fell for Trippy. Then he called me on my cell. Andrea we talked and are working things out. Girl he fell for me as hard as I fell for him. He wants a relationship with me. I'm so siked, slow down Sandra, slow down. Andrea I'm having Sunday dinner and you're invited. You really want me there. Yeah girl if it hadn't been for you taking me to the wedding we might not have met. So Andrea be at my house on Sunday at 4:300 pm.

Then Sandra called Brenda. Ring, ring, hello, hello Sandra what's up. Girl you're never going to guest who's coming to Sunday dinner with us. With us, who? You Brenda, Andrea, the kids and my Mom and. Who girl? Who's coming to dinner? Brian The Bill Collector! Nah you got to be kidding. Brenda he called and we talked and we are working things out. Well I'll be, I never thought that it would happen. God is good, God is so good! Brenda I'm so happy and excited at the same time. I need you to come and help me get ready for my Sunday dinner. We only have two days to prepare. Sandra that's plenty of time. I'll be over this evening so we can plan a menu.

Knock, knock Trippy runs to the door and looks out. It's Aunt Brenda Nanny. Trippy let her in. Hello kids. Hi Aunt Brenda. Sandra walks out. In the living room. What's up girl? What's up with you Sandra? You sure are glowing. He really has an effect on you. I can't wait to meet him myself. You will just wait until Sunday.

Brenda I really want to make an impression on him. So I want to prepare a nice tasty meal. You know they say "a way to a man's heart is through his stomach." I want this meal to be unforgetful. Well what do you want to fix. I was thinking about having prime ribs, potatoes and a vegetable medley with hot homemade rolls and butter.

I also want to serve some tasty appetizers. I will have mini crab cakes, wings, a vegetable and a fruit tray. For dessert I want to serve chocolate mousse and sweet potato cheese cake topped off with a sweet tea. Sandra that's a bomb dinner. He's going to enjoy that. I need yawl at the house help me. And Brenda don't stare too hard! You know how you do. Sandra do you want me there or not? I'm not going to be staring at him. But you did say he was fine as wine. Girl, he is, he really is.

SUNDAY DINNER

By Sunday morning Sandra was a nervous wreak. She had prep everything on Saturday night. Her home was immaculate. Sandra put out her best china. She had fresh flowers on the table. Her place looked fit for a king. She thought he will be my king very soon.

Next she had to find something nice to wear. While looking through her closet she found her black form fitting dress. You can't go wrong with black she thought. I think I'll wear this she said while smiling. This would make him crazy with desire seeing her in that dress. It fit her body like a glove an accented every curve on her body. Sandra was built like a brick house any way. She simple was also very gorgeous. Even though she didn't have a man before Brian came into her life, she made sure that she stayed in shape and kept her hair and nails done. Her motto was just because you're doing bad, you don't have to look bad!

Her Dinner was done by 3:00. Sandra went through her home to make sure everything was just right. Her powder room was cleaned, smelling good and stocked with all the necessary things. Her dining room was set up perfect; with all of her fine china set at her table. The candy dishes were filled with chocolates and the appetizer platter were ready to be used. She even had champagne and wine cooling. Brenda came over for a last inspection. Girl your really did good. Thanks Brenda. I'm still a little bit nervous. Sandra drink a small glass of wine to calm your nerves. Only if you have one with me.

61

Sandra and Brenda drank a small glass of red wine. It was nice and chilled. The chimes on the clock began to ring. Oh it's 4:00 p.m. Brenda I need to get dressed and make sure the Boys are dressed. By 4:20 everyone was dressed and waiting for Brian to come. Fives minutes later Andrea and Sandra's mother arrived.

Everyone was dressed and looking good for Brian. Sandra told Trippy and the boys not to ask too many questions, because she didn't want them to scare him away. She wanted them to make a good first impression.

Finally at five on the dot the door bell rings. Of course Trippy was the one who went to the door. He opened the door and tells him to come in. Trippy says it is the Bill Collector, Nanny! Brenda's mouth dropped opened. Brenda whispered under her breath, that Brian was finer than what Sandra had described to her. Sandra nervously walks over to Brian and said "welcome to my home, Brian come in". Brian was carrying a shopping bag and a bouquet of red roses. He walks to Sandra and gives her a kiss on her cheek and hands her the roses. These are for you. Hello everyone I'm Brian. He looks at Andrea and said it so nice to see you again Andrea. She smile and said you too. Then Brian said I have a little some thing for you all. He gave Brenda, Andrea and Sandra's grandmother a box of chocolates. He gave Trippy a hand held game and each one of the boys an X-boy game. Everyone seemed to be very pleased and impressed with him. They were all mesmerized by Brian's charm.

Oh I forgot the appetizers, Sandra said. Anyone want any? I do said Trippy. Wait honey let me serve my guest first. After everyone had the appetizers. The group went into the family room so that Sandra could get the dinner ready. Brian sat in the family room with Sandra's grandmother, while Andrea and Brenda helped her in the kitchen. Girl you didn't say he was that fine said Brenda. Oh yes I did. I couldn't help but stare Sandra.

Sandra you better hold onto him. He's got manners and is nice too! But why is he single? You need to find out. I want to know why a fine stallion with manners is still single. What is he hiding? Girl you better find out. Hush Brenda. Don't go starting. I'll get all the information from him, and you know I'll tell you.

Finally dinner was served. Everyone sat down at the table. Her dinner table sat twelve. Trippy asked to say the grace. He told everyone to bow their heads and close their eyes.

"God is good and God is great and we thank you for the food that my Nanny prepared. And thank you God for Mr. Brian, The Bill Collector, Amen". Everyone said Amen!

Brian seemed to be enjoying his meal. He looked at Sandra and said my compliments to the chef. Sandra looked at him with a loving smile and said thank you. The boys and Trippy fell in love with Brian right from the start. Sandra's grandmother liked him too. She always had her opinion about who her granddaughter dated. Brian really made a good impression on her.

After dinner, the food was put up and the kitchen was cleaned up; then all of the adults went back into the family room. Brenda said let's watch TV. The movie classic "Lady Sings the Blues" is on tonight. Yeah that a good one. I haven't seen that in years said Andrea . . . I want to see it too said Brenda and Brian.

Well Lady sings the blues is it.

Let pop some pop corn and get the wine. Sandra popped the pop corn and got the wine. The boys went into their room to play their video games.

The movie came on and everyone got comfortable. Sandra snuggled up against Brian and the other ladies settled onto the other sofa. This movies brought back many memories for everyone. After awhile everyone was sobbing. Brian pulled Sandra closed to him.

AS usual Billy Dee Williams was the man. When Billy said to Diana Ross *"what is love without someone to share it with"*, you could have heard a pin drop. The ladies were afraid to look at the love birds. But Brian and Sandra were both feeling this movie. No one hardly ate any pop corn. But they did drink the wine. The wine was very good. It was light and not too dry or sweet.

Once the movie was over Andrea and Brenda got up. Time to go we have work tomorrow. They thanked Sandra Michelle for the lovely meal and said goodnight to Brian. Sandra's Grandmother Mrs. Elaine said it was time for her to go too. She called the boys to let them know she was leaving. They came running out and they gave her kisses. We love you Grand mom. I love you too she replied. Grand mom looked at Brian, told him she was glad to meet him. She then told him to be good to her granddaughter. Brian got up and gave Grand mom Elaine a big hug and said I will.

Brian and Sandra sat back down. He looked into Sandra's eyes, took her hands and said *"Sandra I really like you a lot. I think I'm falling in love with you."* tears were running down her face. He wiped her tears away and said don't cry. I thought I had lost you for not being up front with you! I thank you for not giving up on me.

Oh Brian, finally I feel like I've found real happiness. Brian I think about you all of the time. You know even when I first saw you as the Bill Collector, I started thinking and dreaming about you. Even when I took my showers your face would appear on the glass, and even when I was driving I would see your face in my mirror. There were nights when I woke up in cold sweats thinking about you! This was in spite of all the harassing phone calls and harassing house visits.

As he held her in his arms, Brian looked at Sandra very lovingly and said Sandra Michelle, I am sorry for what I put you through. But I am very happy that we are together now!

And Brian after all of that, you have to be the one. I feel it in my bones. Brian I am sorry that you had to go through all the deceitfulness. But I am glad you are with me now. He pulled her close to him and then gives her a very passionate kiss! Then he said, "baby I want to spend the rest of my life with you"! Brian I feel the same way about you and you are the one! I really know and feel that you are the one!

He looks at his watch and said I guess it's time for me to go home, I have to be at work early tomorrow.

Sandra walks him to the door, they kiss, he said I'll call you.

Sandra sits down on the sofa and looks up and said

"Thank you Lord"!

Sandra was on a high like she never felt before. It had been such a long time since she had been involve with anyone. He likes my grandmother and my children and Trippy. My grandmother gives her stamp of approval. When my grandmother approves of a man, he has to be the one. Because she is very hard and critical of men.

She remembers how my ex–husband dogged me. Grand mom vowed that she wouldn't allow it to happen again. Just at that moment the phone rang. It was my grandmother. Sandra he is so cute and nice. Baby he's a keeper. Grand mom I saw you sneaking peeks at him. Hush Sandra I might be old, but I'm not dead. Child, Brian is fine and he seems very nice and he has manners too. He was raised well. I never heard my grandmother call a man cute or even fine. She was old school. Baby he's the one. She told Sandra. Honey he is a keeper. Don't let him get away! Yes Grand mom I won't let him get away. I'm going to hold on tight to him!

Grand mom hold on someone is calling on the other line. Hello, hello Brenda, Sandra he is fine. He is a keeper. Does he have any brothers? Brenda I don't know, but I'll have to call you back, because my grandmother is on the line. Okay hurry and call me back. Hello Grand Mom I have to call you back because I have a call coming in. Okay Sandra I will talk with you tomorrow.

Hello, Sandra, yes Andrea girl I just wanted to tell you Brian is very nice. I didn't really get a chance to interact with him at the wedding, but he seems like a winner. Sandra I'll talk with you later in the week, okay girl thanks for everything. Okay I' ll get with you later, bye, bye.

I need a hot shower, she thought. After showering, just as she was about to get in bed the phone rings. She looks at the called id, it's him. Hi you, she says. Hey baby, how are you. I'm fine. Sandra I wanted to call to let you know I had a great time. I enjoyed your family and friends. I didn't know what to expect. But they made me feel right at home. What are you doing? Brian I just got in bed. Tomorrow I have a big day at work and I need to get my rest. Good night my love. I will talk with you tomorrow. Good night Brian. She hangs the phone up and fall fast asleep.

When Brian called Sandra the next evening, she said she had a question to ask him, but didn't know how he would respond to it. Sandra what is it. You can ask me anything. I don't have anything that I want to hid from you. Okay, Brian, you're so nice, you're handsome, and have a good job. I want to know how come you don't have someone in your life? Or do you? Is there someone you haven't told me about? Brian you just seem to be too good to be true. Brian paused and then his voice started to crack. Sandra wondered to herself if she should be concerned.

Then Brian said, Sandra I was married and my wife was killed in a car accident. Oh Brian I'm so sorry. Sandra she was in a car pool, and while riding home from work one day a guy came driving down the wrong side of the highway and hit the car head on. Everyone in the car were killed, including the driver of the other car. I tried not to think about it. It's been three years now. I never thought I would get over it. She was my childhood sweet heart. We had just started talking about starting a family when that happened. My wife died on impact. There were three others in the car, who lasted a few weeks before they past away.

I thought my life was over. I felt so empty. I didn't know what to do with myself. So that I didn't go crazy I got involved in my work. Maybe that's why you felt I was being a pest. I probably was taking my frustrations out on you. I tried not to think about the accident. I was angry, depressed and frustrated for a very long time. I didn't think I would ever get over it. I had made a vow to myself that I would never get involved in another relationship! It hurts too much to lose someone you love. It was a very sad and low period in my life. There were several women who tried to start a relationship with me. But I didn't have an interest in them. I started watching television ministries to help me try and get over my loss. Little by little I started coming around.

My family is out on the West coast so I really didn't have anyone to lean on other than my job. My parents are retired and I have three younger brothers, and one sister. I didn't want to go back home and burden my family, so I stayed here and tried to deal with it as best I could. Things have been really rough for me emotionally. I asked God why so many times. Brian I didn't know about your wife. I'm so sorry. You need a hug. When you come over I owe you a big hug. Thanks Honey I needed that.

Sandra you are the first and only woman that I've talked too in three years since the accident. I didn't think I would be ever be able to love again. When I heard Trippy's voice on the phone it melted my heart. I always wanted a son who I could play ball with. Honey you have been a bright spot in my heart. You have helped me to learn to love again. When I think about you my heart skips a beat. When I leave you I can't wait to see you again. I love you and your family. And honey I've always wanted to have children and now I have you and your boys. She smiles to herself, because her clock hadn't run out yet. And there was a possibility if they got married she could have a child for him. She said Mom always said God works in mysterious ways!

Sandra Michelle I sure hope you can love me and will fall in love with me. I can't take another hurt. Brian I do love you. Can I see you tomorrow evening, Sandra Michelle? Yes Brian, I'll cook dinner for you. Thanks, goodnight, goodnight.

After dinner Brian asked Sandra Michelle where her parents were. She told him that her father died when she was in high school. Then she got misty eyes. My mother died two years ago. Brian she was my best friend. She got sick and had to be put in a nursing home. I went to see her every day. Even through her sickness she was up beat. Mother had the warmest and brightest smile. She never said anything bad about anyone. She always she said God was going to send me and the boys someone who would love us unconditionally. She always wished the best for me and my children. Mother told me one day real soon it was going to happen. She said she hoped she would be alive to witness it. But if not we already had her blessings. Even though she was the one sick, she encouraged me every time I saw her. Mother was a very religious person. Her faith in God was so strong. She told me to continue to pray and trust and believe in God. Brian you know God always picks the prettiest flowers for his garden. My mother was one of those flowers. Brian I miss her dearly. You would have loved her and I know she would have loved you.

Mother always told me to ask God for what I wanted. And you know Brian everyday I would pray that God would send me that man of my dreams. Someone who would love me and be in love with. And of course someone who would love my children. Because after all I'm a package deal.

And you know Brian I would draw pictures of the man that I would fall in love with. I would put labels of what I wanted in a man, such as a Christian who loved the Lord, working man, handsome, fun, lover of children and someone who would love us unconditionally. Brian you are that picture that I drew. I will show you my drawings. You really looked liked the face in my pictures. Brian looked in Sandra's eyes and said "honey you are a package deal". And I wouldn't have you any other way. I am so glad that I am the man in your pictures!

Brian my Grandmother has become my mother. She is very protective of me. You made a very good impression on her. Grand mom speaks her mind. If she didn't like you would have known it. My grandmother like you a whole lot.

And you know Brian just when I was about to give up, God sends you into my life. "Thank you Jesus." My grandmother moved back here, when my mother died to help me. And she's been a God send ever since. I come from a fairly large family. I have three sister and two brothers. We are a pretty close family.

Grandmother looks out for all of us. Sometime she can be flip with her lips but she is sweet as pie. We all love grandmother. But one thing I wish was to have my mother here so she could see you. I know she is smiling down from heaven and you have her blessings.

Sandra Michelle, I will do everything to stay in your grandmother, your sons, Trippy and your friends good grace. I love you and don't want to ever lose you. Then they kissed passionately. MMM her lips are very sweet and soft. I think I m going to love this.

DATING

THE FIRST THING BRIAN DID was to join church with Sandra and her family. Sandra found out how spirit filled Brian was. He also loved the Lord. Brian wanted to be involved in every aspect of their lives. He joined the couples group with Sandra at the church. They went to Bible Study every Wednesday evening.

After a while he was able to help her resolve the past due account. No one would ever bother her again. Brian helped Sandra to get all of her bills in order. Everyday he showed her something new. She had to pinch herself over and over again. This seemed almost too good to be true. Sandra helped Brian's numb feelings of his wife's death to dissolve. This brought them even closer.

Brian and Sandra went out every weekend for the next two years. Once a month they did a family outing. Brian loved her boys and grandson. The boys loved Brian too. They loved talking and playing ball with him. This was the first time that they had really been able to interact with a man. He showed them that he wanted eventually for them to be a family. They got to learn everything about each other. Sandra remembered that her mother always told her that action speaks louder then words. Brian really was proving this to them. There wasn't nothing that he wouldn't do for them. He loved all of them very much. Brian is so glad that God put Sandra Michelle in his life and he couldn't wait to become her husband.

ENGAGEMENT

AFTER DATING FOR TWO YEARS Brian felt like it was time to ask Sandra to marry him. He loved her so much and wanted to spend the rest of his life with her and the boys. They were so compatible and so much in love with each other!

He planned to ask her on Valentine's Day which was her birthday. Brian made reservations at Shalimar's Restaurant. When he came to pick Sandra up at her house, he told her that he had something special to share with her. I wondered what it was, what could it be she asked herself. I know today is my birthday, but what could it be she wondered. Dinner was excellent. First appetizers them salad and finally the main course which was a lobster tail dinner. He had the restaurant's finest bottle of wine brought to the table. A group of violinist surround the table and played a medley of love songs to the couple.

Finally the waitress brought out a chocolate cake topped with ice cream. Oom this is so good she said. As Sandra dug into the dessert Brian took her hand and said baby you have made me so happy. You are the total package, honey. She looked at him with tears in her eyes, while her heart beating a mile a minute. Baby you've made me very happy too, she replied.

Then he took her hands. He gently kissed them. Brian took her left hand and kissed it again. Then he took a ring box out opened it, got down on his knees and asked her to marry him. By this time all attention was on this couple. The other patrons in the restaurant were standing up cheering and wishing them their congratulations.

Tears were coming down her face so fast and hard that Sandra didn't see that it was a four carte diamond. The ring had such a bling to it, that it if you looked too long it would blind you. Yes, yes she screamed with joy. Sandra was so loud that everyone in the restaurant began laughing and clapping. After getting her composure, she said yes softly to Brian again.

She whispered yes I'll marry you. He took her in his arms and kissed her. By then everyone in the restaurant stood up and gave them a standing ovation. This looked like a love scene out of the movies. Brian told Sandra he loved her and was in loved with her. Through her tears, she said me too, Brian I love you too.

Sandra told Brian, meeting him was the best day in her life. But this day topped it all. Then she asked Brian how did he know her right ring size. I had the help of your Grandmother and Andrea. They got me one of your rings out of your jewelry box. Then we all went shopping for your ring. Do you like it? Yes I love it. It's perfect!

And you know Sandra before I got the ring I asked your grand mother and your sons permission to marry you. And of course I had to ask my man Trippy. They all said yes. Trippy had the nerve to ask me what took me so long. So here I am! Sandra I'm yours forever and ever.

She had never been happier. This was one of the happiest days in her life.

Sandra couldn't wait to get home to tell the children and Brenda that he proposed. Of course her Grandmother and Andrea already knew that it was going to happen. They were in on the secret. How did the boys keep a secret from me she asked? Sandra that's our secret he said!

Brian told Sandra he had one more secret for her. What Brian, what is it she asked? He took an envelope out of his jacket and handed it to her. When she opened the enveloped Sandra screamed and crumpled in his arms. Is this for real she asked. Yes my love. I knew you haven't been anywhere because of your finances, so I wanted to give you an engagement vacation trip as a present. With the help of your mother and Andrea we got your vacation schedule from work. And we found out you could go on vacation at anytime.

"Sandra I planned our trip to Cancun for next week. We will be leaving on Monday and return the following Monday". But what about my passport.? I don't have one. Then she began to cry. Wipe you tears honey that was taken care of months ago. I happen to be on top of things he said. Now that you have me in you life you won't have to worry about anything any more. That also includes the children. I want to be their daddy. All she could do was fall into Brian's arms and weep tears of joy. Once she composed herself he said lets go home.

It had been years since Sandra had been this happy. She felt like she was dreaming. It seemed to good to be true. She had never been out of the country. Now everything that she ever wanted was happening for her. She looks up to the shy and said "Thank You Lord, Thank You!

CANCUN

BRIAN WAS THE TOTAL PACKAGE. He knew how to treat a lady. He had brought Sandra a whole new wardrobe. He packed everything that she needed. All she had to do was be ready to leave with him. She and the children were so excited. The boys and Trippy were so happy for her. They had come to love Brian. He had gotten involved in every aspect of their lives. Brian really made them feel so good. Brian went to all of their games and practices. He even went to their school conference meetings with Sandra.

Brian pulled up in a limousine to take Sandra to the airport. They were flying into Atlanta and then on to Cancun Mexico. Sandra had never been out of the country. She was very excited and a little bit apprehensive. She didn't know what to expect. But once they landed all her fears went out of the window. Cancun was very hot but oh so beautiful.

Once they arrived at their private villa all she could do was cry. It was one of the most beautiful places that she ever saw. There was a balcony that they could stand on and lookout and see the country side. And they even had their own private beach with an in ground pool. Sandra looked at Brian and said I don't have a bathing suit. He looked back at her and said no you don't, you have three bathing suits. And Sandra I even brought the sun screen. So stop worrying honey everything is going to be alright.

Brian had a whole itiniery planned for her. Everyday and night they had something planned. Dinner, dancing, sailing, scuba diving, sightseeing, touring and more.

On their last evening at the restaurant Brian had a special song, "when a man loves a woman" serenaded to her, by the group that was performing at the restaurant. What a special treat this was for her. Sandra thought this was the end of the surprises. But Brian had one more surprise. He took the mike from the lead singer and took Sandra's hand and began to sing. You are my lady, you're everything that I've been living for and I promised to love you more each day, because you're all that I need. Tears of joy flowed down her face. Everyone in the restaurant clapped and whistled. Brian turns to Sandra and confesses his love to her. Sandra Michelle you have made me so happy. You have made me feel like living again. Sandra Michelle I want you to know that I also prayed for God to send me someone special. I am so grateful that he sent you to me!

Sandra was bursting all over inside. She also had a wonderful voice. She wanted to sing something to Brian. She asked him to give her the mike. Sandra burst out singing "I am telling you that you are best thing that ever happened to me, and I am not living without you, not living without I don't want to be free of you, no, no, no way, I am living without you" Oh Brian you're the best thing that happened to me. The other guest in the restaurant went crazy as she sang to him. They gave Sandra a standing ovation. Brian pulled her closed to him and gave her a passionate kiss. Then he looked at Sandra and said what other surprises do you have. She started blushing and said that's it.

What a time they had. Brian this is the most beautiful thing that you've done for me. You have made me oh so happy. Brian replied I will do everything to give you the happiness you have shown me. Sandra Michelle I have one more surprise for you. Before we go home we will go to my parent's home in California. I've talked about you so much they wanted to meet you right away. Brian I'm nervous. I hope they will like me. Sandra Michelle stop worrying. They'll love you just like I do. Come here. He gives her a hug and said everything going to be alright.

Once they got through the airport in California, Brian's whole family was waiting at baggage check. Hi mom, hi dad. Brian, Brian. All of his family surrounded him. You would have thought a celebrity had arrived. Then his parents turned to Sandra and said you must be her, Sandra. We've heard so much about you. Then his parents gave her a hug and kiss. This really helped to erase her fears.

The group walked towards the waiting van to go to Brian's parents home. Everyone took to Sandra like they had known her all of their lives. They liked her and she liked them. His parents thanked Sandra for helping their son love again. They had been worried for him ever since the death of his wife. They didn't think he would ever find love again. Meeting her made them very happy.

Brian's parents welcomed Sandra and told her they would be proud to have her for a daughter in law.

WEDDING PLANS

BRIAN WE NEED TO TALK with the pastor. I know he would want us to have marital counseling. They both met with Pastor Dennis. He set up a ten week session for them. They would meet every Wednesday at 6:00 pm. Sandra and Brian were each given a marriage book that they would have to read and study. They would each have to do the weekly assignments and discuss them the following week. The sessions were very helpful. Many times you think you know someone until you live with them. The sessions also dealt with children, finances, feelings, love and sex. It was embarrassing at first but after the second session they were laughing and happy that they were having the counseling sessions. The sessions allowed them to grow closer to each other.

Sandra had so many friends. She wanted all of them to be a party of her wedding. She would have eight Brides Maids, one Maid of Honor and Two Matron of Honors. Each friend held a special place in her life. Brian's sister Amirah would be her junior brides maid. And of course she needed a group of friend to help coordinate the wedding. They only had 12 months to plan.

What color did she want and what kind of dresses and shoes would she and her bridal party wear. How would they wear their hair?

After assembling her wedding party, Sandra had a dinner meeting to discuss her plans. She set up a schedule of meeting so that everyone would be on the same page. The meetings were once month at her sister's house.

She also had an activity planned every two months so that the girls would be in concert with one another. These meetings were fun times for them. The girls gave her all of the support she needed. Everyone was very happy for Sandra. This was a longtime coming.

David Bridal was the wedding salon that was chosen. After showing the girls the dresses that she like, she made plans for everyone to go and try on their dresses. Of course the color they all agreed on was a lavender color, which was Sandra's favorite color. This was so exciting to everyone, as they selected their dresses. But the real joy was seeing Sandra in her wedding gown. It was magnificent, simply breath taking.

This was a very happy group, everyone seemed to be on one accord. You know it's very difficult to work in harmony with such a large group. But this group did everything in love for Sandra.

They began to go to all of the Bridal shows to get ideas. The shows had all kinds of prizes the bride to be could win. Sandra won her bridal bouquet and wedding day make up at one of the shows.

Katrina her niece would be the Maid of Honor and Andrea and her cousin Lynn were her Matrons of honor. Brenda said Andrea's deceased husband was smiling in heaven, because he loved Sandra like a sister. Eight of her child hood friends were chosen as brides maids.

Everyone seemed to be so happy for Sandra; it had been a very long time since she's had happiness in her life. Her friends wanted to do everything to make sure that everything went off perfectly.

The wedding party all agreed to have Sandra's wedding shower party at the Hilton Hotel. Sandra was such a loving and giving person, and they wanted to show the same kind of love to her. She knew so many people and they were receiving calls from many of them asking to be put on the invite list.

Time was winding down. Two more months and the day would finally be here. She ordered the flowers and wedding cakes. Sandra has so many friends that she had to have two receptions. One would at the country club and at the other one would be in the church's reception hall.

She wanted to give Brian something special for a wedding gift. But what could she get him that would be memorable. She asked Andrea and Brenda her two best friends to think of something memorable. They both said a bracelet that had "The Bill Collector" engraved on it. This would be the perfect gift for Brian. That's a good idea she said. That outstanding bill she owed was the reason why we met in the first place.

Sandra, Andrea and Lynn went to jeweler's row to find the perfect bracelet for Brian. The Diamond Palace had the perfect bracelet. It was platinum and gold. Ivan the jeweler said he would be able to engrave the words "The Bill Collector" on it. He would also have diamonds put on the beginning of each word for a total of three diamonds equaling one carat.

Tears starting falling, because whenever she thought about the past it brought back memories. They were stressful times that turned into something positive. Andrea and Lynn took Sandra into their arms and gave her a big sisterly hug. Honey everything going to be alright. You have all that you need, a man who loves you, a wonderful family and the best friends in the world who also loves you. So stop your crying and be happy. Sandra looks at her girlfriends and said "I'm very happy these are tears of joy and happiness. They are also tears of freedom. I don't have to look over my shoulders anymore.

BRIDAL SHOWER

FINALLY THE DAY HAD COME. The Wedding party had done an excellent job in setting up for the shower. Everyone was in place waiting for Sandra to arrive. Of course Trippy was the one who brought her in. Trippy really kept this secret from Sandra. What a surprise it was. She really was surprise. Then comes the tears. Everyone knew by now that Sandra was a crier. As she walked in Sandra noticed on the wall was a large beautiful plaque with a picture of Sandra saying congratulations. This brought Sandra to tears again. Wow, she said this is beautiful. Where did you get my picture she asked. Oh we got it, and that all matter someone shouted! As she walked around the room and saw the cake which was so beautiful with her picture on it she got misty eyes.

Sandra broke down and cried when she saw Brian's mother, sister and Aunts there. They had traveled all the way from California for the Bridal Shower. Brian's mother and her family had come two weeks early because they were hosting the rehearsal dinner. This would be a surprise for Sandra.

They would tell her after the Bridal Shower was over.

The bridal party had been set up for 100 people. All the guest who were invited attended the Bridal shower. There were a few more people who weren't invited who also came as well. This was a very happy occasion.

Katrina and Lynn asked everyone to take their seats so that they could be served lunch. Sandra said she wanted to say the grace. She asked everyone to join hands.

Father God I want to thank you for this day. I thank you for all my Bridal Party Members, family and friends who have gather here today at my shower to help celebrate my up coming marriage. I thank you for all of my family and friends who also traveled near and far to attend my shower. Then Father we thank you for the food that has been prepared for the nourishment of our bodies. Father blessed this day and everyone present. We give you thanks. Amen.

Sandra got so many beautiful gifts. The lingerie gifts were the hit of the shower. After looking at all of the lingerie, she asked when will I have time to wear all of this. Some of her guest shouted out, oh you will. Sandra began to cry after reading some of the very touching cards. She just couldn't believe that her dream was finally coming true.

They ate, played games and continued to open gifts and of course talked about the Bill Collector, the man that Sandra would soon be marrying. One of her guest said I want a Bill Collector. Does he have any brothers or friends? No she replied. His brothers are too young and he's the one and only Bill Collector. All of the guest burst out laughing.

Everyone was given a small bottle of champagne and a miniature edible wedding cake commemorating her special day. Sandra was so excited because her college roommates and school buddies had attended the shower. She hadn't seen them in a few years. This really did her heart good. She couldn't ask for more.

FINAL PREPARATIONS

SANDRA AND BRIAN WERE SO in love and learned to do everything together. They met with the photographer, who came highly recommend. He showed them photo books of weddings that he had done. He said he would do both the pictures and the video as well. And the price was right. It's just what they had figured in their budget. Even thought Brian was paying for everything, they wanted to make sure everything was what they had discussed in their budget.

They worked out the details and time for the photographer to be at the hotels to take pictures of the bridal party.

Sandra and Brian finally found a DJ that they liked. Sandra gave the DJ a list of the songs they wanted played at their wedding. She told him she wanted to make sure everyone loved the music and dance. They wanted a jamming party at their wedding. The last thing they had to do was find a band to play at the cocktail hours. After interviewing several bands they found the one that they wanted. (The Soul Sounds Jazz Band).

Sandra and Brian went to lunch so that they could finalize details of their up coming wedding. They were pleased as they looked over their schedule while checking items off. They had to add a few more flowers to their list because Sandra forgot their Godmothers. But that wasn't really a big deal. The florist was loving Sandra for her business. She provided extra butineers for the guys and extra corsages for female guest.

Brian and his guys had all been fitted with their tuxedos, shoes and accessories. The guys were ready to walk down the aisle for their boy Brian!

Sandra had seen a chocolate machine at one of the bridal shows. After talking with her Bridal Party they decided that it was too messy. They didn't want anyone to get their clothes messed up. So Sandra decided to go with the ice sculpture. The ice would be sculptured into large a heart with both of their names engraved in the center of it.

Finally the time had come. The day before everyone would meet at the church for the rehearsal. It was a very good rehearsal. After it was over they all went into the church fellowship hall for dinner. Brian mother really had a beautiful spread for them. After dinner the bridal party mingled and helped to put finishing touches on the church reception hall.

It was late when everyone headed back to the hotel. Sandra was sleepy but she couldn't sleep because of the excitement of the upcoming wedding the next day.

WEDDING

THE DAY HAD FINALLY COME when she will marry the man of her dreams. Sandra was beaming and glowing at the same time. She stood and looked up to the heavens and whispered mother I wish you were here. As she said that a double rainbow went across the sky. It was so beautiful. She knew it was a sign from her mother. Her mother loved rainbows.

The morning air was sweet and bright. The women in the wedding party stayed at the Hilton Hotel. The guys all stayed at the Clarion Hotel. Everyone arose bright and early to have their faces done by the makeup artist.

After getting dressed the photographed had all of the girls to assemble in the hotel lobby in front of the baby grand piano. My what a beautiful sight. The girls were all so lovely, from the flower girls to the maids and maids of honor. The hotel guest were admiring them and giving them beautiful compliments.

After the photo session, the wedding bus arrived to take the bridal party to the church. The bus picked the groomsmen up first. The men all looked very handsome in their tuxedos. Then the bus went and picked the ladies up and little girls. A stretch limo came and picked up Sandra and her maid of honor and two matrons of honor.

As the wedding party waited outside the church, a brief thunder storm started up. Then all of a sudden the sun shone so bright and another rainbow appeared. A second rainbow appeared across the sky. It to was so beautiful. And the storm was over. Three rainbows appearances in one day she knew that this was a sign from her mother to get on with her life with Brian.

Sandra smiled and whisper thank you mother for your approval and blessings. All was well. Sandra was so happy because truly this was the day that the Lord has made. While waiting in the limo she saw so many family and friends that she hadn't seen in a very long time.

Brian's Godmother and Sandra's Aunt were escorted to their seats.

Then Brian's mother and Sandra's sister-in-law were escorted in. They both lit a candle on the candelabra at the alter. The candle on the left is for the bride and candle on the right is for the groom. This represents the couple as individual and that their lives at that moment. They are two distinct individuals who will become one.

Mike an usher who was a family friend, ushered Sandra Michelle's Grandmother Elaine in. She had a smile on her face that could light up the world. Today her baby girl would find the happiness that she has yearned for!

The three flower girls were so cute as they dropped their petals.

The audience roared with laughter at Trippy, who was the ring boy. He came running in fast. Trippy ran straight to Brian and stood beside him and waited for his Nanny to come in.

When Amirah the Junior Brides Maid walked in, the crowd just oohed and oohed at how gorgeous she looked.

The bridal party came in on "Step in the name of Love". Everyone in the bridal party was in step, and no one missed a beat. This routine really got the crowd going.

Sandra's coordinator Joanna came to the Limo and asked was she ready. It's time to go in the church.

As she was being helped out of the car, passersby were admiring how beautiful she looked; while wondering who she was.

When the song isn't she lovely began to play, Sandra oldest son Michael walked her halfway in and her other two sons (Wayne and Anthony) walked Sandra in the rest of the way. What a beautiful sight! Once they got to the alter "At Last" was song by one of the soloist. What a beautiful program so far.

Sandra had a Friendship bouquet made up of yellow roses. After one of Sandra's closest girl friends Maxine read what friendship was:

> *(A friend is a priceless gift that can't be bought or sold.*
> *A friend is someone you can go too when things are rough.*
> *They lend their heart, ears and shoulders without judging.*
> *They are someone you can count on no matter what the*
> *problem is and offers a helping hand. They also share happy*
> *times together. They care about you and your family.*
> *A true friend loves you unconditionally. Friendship is a value*
> *that is far greater than gold. Gold is cold and lifeless.*
> *But true friendship brings comfort, joy and real love).*

These friends names were called out and 30 of her closest friends came up and received a yellow rose.

They had three Reverends to perform their ceremony. Sandra's Pastor, Brian's Pastor and Sandra's brother who was a pastor. It was such an ecumenical vision having the three pastor working in unison at their wedding ceremony. Each Pastor took a special part in the ceremony.

Before the ceremony started a soloist came up and sang Ribbon in the sky. As he sang there wasn't a dry eye in the church.

One interesting part in the ceremony was the tasting of the four elements (lemon, vinegar, cayenne pepper and honey) that the couples had to partake in to show their love for one another. The four elements symbolizes the promise to love for better or worse, for richer for poorer in sickness and in health. The four elements represents the sour, the bitter the hot and the sweet times of marriage.

The elements were placed on a crystal plate positioned in correspondence to the four directions. Four is the number associated with the base of the pyramid, which is the symbol of a strong foundation.

Brian and Sandra began tasting the elements, beginning with the lemon. Marriage involves individual sacrifice, so that two people harmonize as one. But sacrifice can sometime cause a sour taste in your mouth. The first element would be the lemon so that they could experience the sour taste. Sometimes there is some bitterness in the marriage. So the next taste would be the vinegar. Then the couple tasted the cayenne pepper to experience a heated explosion. After tasting the cayenne pepper Brian and Sandra's eyes started to water. It's said if couples can weather all of these all of the difficult times and still be friends and lovers they will come to understand the sweetness that's in all the previous three elements. This will allow them to taste the sweetness of the honey.

While Sandra and Brian was tasting the elements, there wasn't a dry eye again in the church. There were so many sobs of joy and happiness. Many guest were whispering how beautiful and blessed that part of the ceremony was.

Many of her friends participated in the ceremony by reading the scriptures, and singing solos. Finally the couple said their vows. Then Brian said vows to her three sons and Trippy. He promised to love and cherish them forever. And he promised to always be there for them. There wasn't a dry eye in the church after his vows to the family. What a beautiful honor. Then the bridal party, family members, and anyone who wanted too, took communion. As the couple knelt at the alter the bridal party, family and friends surrounded them.

Finally all three Pastors pronounced them man and wife. The couple kissed jumped the broom and proceeded out side of the church. One guess wanted to know why they jumped the broom. Pastor Dennis said that it symbolizes leaving the past behind and the beginning of entering into a new beginning making a loving and happy home together.

People were still crying tears of joy. There wasn't a dry eye at the church. It was one of the most beautiful weddings that we ever saw. Once everyone was outside the church and bunch of white doves were released to the skies. The doves made a heart formation that was so beautiful. Then a plane flew over leaving a message in the sky,

Congratulations "Sandra and Brian"!

What a perfect day was uttered over and over again by their friends. She looks so beautiful. What a beautiful day. I know her mother is singing and shouting in heaven. This is truly the day that The Lord made! Oh happy day. These were the comments that continued to be whispered.

Sandra had so many friends that she had to have two receptions. One for the church and the other for family and friends. The wedding party went to the reception hall in the church to greet the guest. There were about 150 fifty people at the church reception hall. The guest feasted on Cornish Hens, wild rice and a vegetable medley. There was a beautiful three tier cake. The wedding party had decorated the hall so beautifully. It was picture perfect. Each table was decorated with beautiful floral arrangements and a wedding token for each guest.

After dinner the DJ began playing some jamming songs for the guest. Sandra and Brian Danced to the electric slide with the guest. Slide to the left slide to the right, everyone was having a blast dancing. After a champagne toast the wedding party left to go take pictures in the park.

What a beautiful day for picture taking. The park was beautiful with water fountains and beautiful gardens of flowers. The sun shone bright in the clear blue sky. And picture after picture was taken. Once the photographer was finished, everyone got back into the cars and rode to the hotel for the reception.

The reception was in full swing when they arrive. The jazz band was singing all of the latest songs. The band was a real treat for the guest. The guest were eating hor dor ves, drinking and dancing to the band. There was so much to eat and drink. The bar was open for the entire five hour reception. It was simply amazing.

After about one and half hour the guest went upstairs to the formal ballroom. The bridal party had returned from taking pictures. The ballroom décor was simply magnificent. It took your breath away. The wedding party lined up outside the dining room so they could be formally introduced to their guest. The bridal party were lined up on a spiral staircase that seemed like it was in the heavens. They looked so beautiful.

Finally it was time for the Newly Weds to enter.

Will everyone please stand and greet Mr. & Mrs. Brian Williams for the very first time. It seemed liked they floated in down the staircase as everyone clapped and cheered. You could see the happiness on their faces.

As they took their seats Brian had a special guest come in and sing "At last" to Sandra. This brought tears to Sandra's eyes. What a beautiful surprise.

When dinner was served they feasted on lobster tail, baked salmon and lemon chicken, wild rice, a vegetable medley, rolls and butter. The dinner was hot and very tasty.

Once the maid of honor gave her toast the best man got up and gave his toast. It was one of the most romantic and thought provoking toast that had ever been done. It was one of the highlights of the reception. It gave everyone something to think about. Everyone who commented on the toast were totally surprised as well as please to have heard it. The wedding couple also enjoyed his toast. Love was certainly in the air.

For desert each guest was served a strawberry parfait that was to die for. The newly weds dance their first song, to "Just One Life Time" by Jay Black foot and "forever that how long I'm going to love you" Sandra serenaded Brian. Then the bridal party came up and danced. After that, the party was on. Everyone got up and dance to the DJ's magic. He was so great and played song after song. Everyone in the room were on their feet. The music brought back memories and some old dance moves. It was a happy time had by all. The DJ was rocking. He had everyone up on their feet. He played peculator, you drop the bomb on me, you and me girl, it take two, let me clear my throat, flash light, stay in my corner, joy and pain, square business all night long, and on and on and on. This was a real party.

This was a party. Each one of Sandra's sons danced with her. And of course Trippy dance with her as well. Brian picked him up so they both could dance with Trippy.

Brian began singing Just One Life Time To Sandra, that it won't be long enough. This caused the tears to flow. Because she said she wouldn't get married until she song that song or had someone sing this song to her. This was like a dream come true.

Joanna had all of the single ladies come to the floor. Sandra threw the bouquet and one of her girlfriends caught it. Brian's nephew caught the garter. Trippy had so much fun that he wore himself out.

Thank you God, you are an awesome God!

The boys would be staying with Grand mom while Sandra and Brian honeymooned. They were leaving for Montego Bay Jamaica early Sunday Morning. After the last guest had said there goodbyes this happy couple has their limo driver take them back to their room at the Hilton. They were so happy and exhausted that they collapsed on their King size Bridal bed and fell asleep! What a Happy ending to a beautiful ceremony. This is a blessed welcome to a long and happy life for Brian and Sandra Michell Williams.

BIBLE VERSES TO LIVE BY:

No weapon formed against me shall not prosper	Isaiah 54:17
All things are possible	Luke 18:27
I will give you rest	Matthews 11:28-30
I love you	John 3:6 & John 3:34
My grace is sufficient	11 Corinthian 12:9 & Psalm 91:15
I will direct your steps	Proverbs 3:5-6
You can do all things through Christ	Philippians 4:13
I am able	11 Corinthian 9★
It will be worth it	Romans 8:28
I will supply all of your needs	Philippians 4:19
I have not given you a spirit of fear	11 Timothy 1:7
Cast all your care on me	1 Peter 5:7
I give you wisdom	1 Corinthian 1:30
I will never leave you or forsake you	Hebrews 15:5
Train up a child in the way he should go	Proverbs 22:6
Make your request be made known	Philippians 4:6
Who can find a virtuous woman	Proverbs 31:10
When you worry	Matthew 6:19-34
When your faith needs stirring	Hebrew 11
When you are lonely and fearful	Psalm 23
For the secret to happiness	Colossians 3:12-17
If your pocketbook is empty	Psalm 37

Songs to sing to help you get through

My God is an awesome God

Great is thy faithfulness

Overflow

Oh Happy Day

You are a Great God

I don't Mind Waiting

He's A wonder in My Soul

Miracles Still Happen

I've Been Redeemed

Come to the Alter

I won't Complain

Precious Lord take My Hand

Blessed Assurance

He's the Captain of My Ship

Things to do if you are being harassed by annoying phone calls from rude bill collectors and tell markers

1. Ask them not to call you and ask them to send everything in writing to you.

2. Get a name of the person who is calling.

3. Get a supervisor or manager's name.

4. If they are being rude hang up.

5. Get your name put on the don't call list.

6. If you have caller id, don't answer the call.

7. Make sure it is your bill.

8. Go over the bill several times with a fine tooth comb. Make sure they didn't charge you more than once.

ABOUT THE AUTHOR

Suzy Q retired from the Atlantic City Superior Court of New Jersey after being employed there for 30 1/2 years of service.

Suzy Q has a BA in history with a minor in Criminal Justice from Montclair State University of New Jersey, and she has a MA degree in Human Resources Training and Development from Seton Hall University in Orange, New Jersey. She moved to Concord, North Carolina in February 2100, with her husband Lawrence. Suzy Q wanted to be able to devote more time to writing her novels. However upon arriving in Concord, she enrolled in the PhD Program with Capella University. She is majoring in the Clinical Counseling Studies Program. At this time she is very busy multitasking with two endeavors as well as being a wife to her loving husband and their dog Jade.

Suzy Q also is a member and attends Simpson Gillespie United Methodist Church in Charlotte North Carolina, she has been recently nominated as Chairperson of the Evangelism Committee.

This is Suzy Q's second novel. All of her upcoming novels will be focused on Health issues. However this book deals with money problems that she feels is very relatable and important to talk about. Today so many people are suffering and faced with money issues; especially right now during this economic crisis. Because so many people are out of work and can not pay their debts on time or at all, they are being harassed by an arrogant Bill Collector. It is Suzy Q's hope that all of her novels can be a benefit by helping someone who is going through something. It is her wish that they will read something that could help with their issue or steer them in the right direction. Suzy Q uses a Christian base for her story-line, because she knows that prayer changes things.

She knows how good God has been to her. All Suzy Q has for God is Total Praise.